A DANGEROUS QUEST

Janet's sister Alison had gone to work in Madeira, but Janet grew concerned when she had not heard from her for several weeks. Against her boyfriend's advice, she decides to go to the island to find out what is wrong. When she discovers that Alison has mysteriously disappeared, she sets out to find her. Janet becomes increasingly attracted to handsome José Perestrelo, the grandson of Alison's employer, but does he know more about her sister's disappearance than he admits?

Books by Dee Wyatt
in the Linford Romance Library:

THE GOLDEN WEB
FUGITIVE LOVE
SPRING WILL FOLLOW

DEE WYATT

◆

A DANGEROUS QUEST

Complete and Unabridged

LINFORD
Leicester

First published in Great Britain

First Linford Edition
published 1997

Copyright © 1993 by Dee Wyatt
All rights reserved

British Library CIP Data

Wyatt, Dee
  A dangerous quest.—Large print ed.—
  Linford romance library
  1. Love stories
  2. Large type books
  I. Title
  823.9′14 [F]

  ISBN 0–7089–5189–9

Published by
F. A. Thorpe (Publishing) Ltd.
Anstey, Leicestershire

Set by Words & Graphics Ltd.
Anstey, Leicestershire
Printed and bound in Great Britain by
T. J. International Ltd., Padstow, Cornwall

This book is printed on acid-free paper

1

"**W**ELL, Janet, do you agree or not?" The managing editor of the local, weekly paper rapped his question from across the table.

Janet Robinson jerked her head suddenly and faced the rebuke on the intelligent, pale face of her employer. His expression, normally calm and businesslike, revealed some impatience as he waited for her answer.

"Sorry, Ralph, what did you say?" Janet swung blue eyes to meet his.

Ralph Johnson, a handsome man somewhere in his mid-sixties and with a distinguished touch of silver in his hair, repeated his question. "I said, do you agree that Morton takes over your column while you are in Madeira?" His level gaze held hers critically and his tone still held a note of controlled impatience.

"Oh, yes — absolutely — I agree entirely — "

"Then that's settled. How much leave do you think you'll need? A week? Two . . . ?"

"I can't say — " Janet knitted her hands into a tight little knot, aware of the thin film of perspiration forming in her palms. "I think two at least. Perhaps three . . . ?"

"Very well! Keep me posted on events." He rose to his feet, his gesture ending the weekly briefing. "Right, that'll do for today. Thank you gentlemen — and lady."

The editorial meeting broke up with its usual babble, leaving Janet — the only woman in the room — stuffing a bundle of papers into her briefcase. Her reflective expression showed none of its usual alertness and her mass of corn-blonde hair was swept back, restrained by a narrow band of black ribbon in a style that enhanced the elegant contours of her face.

One man, Elliott Hanson, remained

behind, waiting for her to gather her things and, as the room emptied, he moved towards her and leaned against the edge of the board-room table.

"What on earth were you day-dreaming about just then?" he asked critically when the last of them had gone. "It's not like you. I thought for a minute that the old man was going to burst a blood vessel."

Janet shrugged philosophically. "I know — and it's really good of him to give me leave like this — especially when so many of the staff are on holiday." She lowered her head, her blue eyes troubled. "It's just that I'm so worried about Alison. I can't seem to concentrate on much else right now."

"Still no word from her?"

Janet shook her head. "No, nothing."

"But five weeks isn't that long to be without a letter, is it? And by all accounts that children's home is pretty remote, stuck on top of a mountain." He gave a small shrug. "Perhaps there's some difficulty collecting the post from up there."

"I don't think so — it certainly hasn't been a problem before."

Ellliot shrugged again. "Well, I shouldn't worry too much. It could be that she's just not got around to writing yet — people do forget sometimes."

"Not my sister!" Janet shook her head again abstractedly. "You know what she's like — efficiency's her middle name. No, Elliott, something's definitely gone wrong and I won't rest until I find out what it is."

"Well, I think you're over-reacting. After all, what's the problem? Alison is over twenty-one. Surely she's old enough to get by without her kid sister clucking away like a mother hen, checking on her movements."

She glanced at him a trifle wearily. Why should it always be so difficult to explain how she felt to Elliott? After all, they were supposed to be a couple, weren't they? Or, at least, they were to everyone else, and it was generally assumed they would get married one day.

Janet sighed, snapping her briefcase shut. "I have a bad feeling about it, that's the problem."

Elliott glanced at her irritably. "I think you're letting your imagination go into over-drive again, Janet, but I don't suppose there'll be any sense out of you until you come back from Madeira — when you've finally found out that all that's happened to your sister is that she's simply forgotten to post off the letters."

Janet felt a sharp flash of anger. It annoyed her when Elliott patronised her like this, treating her as though she was stupid.

She faced him squarely barely containing her temper.

"Alison isn't like that! Not once — in all the time she's been away — has there been a Saturday morning when her letter hasn't dropped through my letter-box."

5

He shrugged. "Well, perhaps she's moved in with this chap she's met — perhaps they've decided to get married — "

Janet interrupted hotly. "She would never do that without telling me! And as far as getting married — " She shook her head. "No, Elliott, it's all wrong!"

Elliott drummed his fingers on the table, regarding her curiously.

"Well, it shouldn't take you too long to flush her out in Madeira. You can cover the place in a day."

Janet frowned thoughtfully, pursing her lips. "I think my best lead will be with Magdalena . . . "

"Magdalena?"

"Alison shared a flat with her in Funchal — and then there's always her boss." She paused, giving a feeble little smile. "He seems a nice old thing. When I telephoned to set up an appointment he kindly suggested sending someone to pick me up from the airport."

6

Elliott grunted audibly. "Thoughtful of him." He moved over to take her hand in his. "Have you booked into a hotel?"

"Yes."

"I don't think I like the idea of you going off like this. I'm not sure that it's such a good idea, an English girl wandering around foreign parts alone — "

Janet smiled. "Haven't you heard, Elliott? Queen Victoria died in 1901, and girls get around quite well these days without a chaperon."

"All the same . . . "

Her smile broadened as she squeezed his hand. "Don't worry about me, Elliott. I can take care of myself."

"So you keep telling me, dear, but I still feel that the sooner we're married, the better."

"I'm not a child, Elliott."

"Perhaps not — in age, that is. But you do tend to get your priorities wrong quite often."

Janet shook her blonde head slowly.

7

"Let's not start quarrelling again, Elliot, please. Can't you understand? I have to see if Alison's all right before I can settle my mind on other things."

"If it isn't this, it would be something else," he grumbled. "You're always making excuses."

His words jogged her conscience. He was right, of course, but she was desperately worried about her sister. After all, they only had each other, having been brought up without parents and been moved around from foster home to foster home since either of them could remember. It was that very fact that had made Alison decide to become a children's nurse in the first place, especially one who could work with homeless kids.

Janet frowned, her blue eyes serious as she remembered the morning Senor Perestrelo's letter had arrived offering her sister a post at his children's home at Camacha, and how quickly Alison had jumped at it.

"But why Madeira?" Janet had

questioned. "Can't you find the same kind of job in this country? There are heaps of homes you could work at near here."

"Why not Madeira, Janet?" Alison had responded defensively. "I've had no experience apart from the training college so Camacha sounds ideal. I believe there are only about twenty children there so it's a wonderful opportunity for me. Don't throw cold water on it, there's a love."

And Janet hadn't thrown cold water on it, but now — oh, how she wished she had.

She glanced up at Elliott, shelving her worries momentarily and turning her thoughts back to the present. Perhaps a little unfairly to Elliott, any thoughts of marriage had been the last thing on her mind these last five weeks. And, if she were to be perfectly honest, they were always somewhere at the bottom of her priority list!

Elliott held her arm as they went through the door. "What shall we do this evening? Any ideas?"

Janet threw him an evasive glance as they stepped into the lift, but made no reply. And, when they reached the ground floor and crossed over to the car park, she said quietly, "There's really no reason for you to come over tonight, Elliott."

"There's every reason," he persisted somewhat impatiently. "I won't see you for weeks."

"Three at the most," she responded, taking refuge in the half truth and unlocking her car. "But I've a lot on my mind right now and I would appreciate an early night. Do you mind?"

"Yes, I do mind." Elliott kissed her forehead, taking his time before adding rather reluctantly, "But, if you insist . . ."

He left her with another small kiss on the cheek and a promise to drive her out to the airport the following day and, as Janet drove home, she chided herself for turning Elliott down the way she did. She owed him some loyalty at least, and she really wasn't fair to him. Sometimes, she wondered why he put up with her indecision at all!

* * *

The next morning, a little after six, Elliott drove Janet out to the airport and, as they walked together towards the gate, he slipped an affectionate arm around her shoulder.

"As soon as you've sorted things out with your sister I want to have a long talk with you."

Janet smiled and looked up at him fondly. "Are you getting impatient?"

"Can you blame me?"

"There's plenty of time."

"Not as much as you think. I've had an offer I can't refuse."

Janet threw him a surprised glance. "What sort of offer?"

He smiled a little smugly. "I was going to keep it as a surprise but I may as well tell you now. You can mull it over while you're away."

11

"What kind of offer?" she asked again.

"Do you remember when you came with me to the Footballers' Presentation dinner and I introduced you to that sports editor, Tom Foster?"

Janet nodded vaguely. "I think so — wasn't he the American?"

"That's the one."

"What about him?"

"He's offered me a job in his Detroit office."

Janet stared at him in astonishment. "Detroit! Detroit, America?"

He nodded. "Detroit, America."

"But what about — ?"

Elliott interrupted her. "You wouldn't believe the salary they're offering, Jan — and the opportunities. I can't turn it down — I'd be a fool if I did. And I think you should know, Janet, that I've already made up my mind to take it whether you want to come or not."

"I see . . ."

"The way I see it, we could get

married and go out there on a kind of working honeymoon. Sounds good, doesn't it?"

A small, icy feeling began to gnaw inside Janet. Living in America with Elliott would be wonderful, she supposed. She would be safe and secure. But, in spite of that supposition, there was something — a vague, intangible reluctance that was drawing her back.

"Well?" Elliott pressed.

Janet shook her head. "I — I don't know ... " Her answer was vague. "It sounds marvellous, of course, but, honestly, Elliott, you have rather thrown it at me, haven't you?"

"I know, and like I said, I intended it as a surprise. But, anyway, think it over while you're in Madeira — there's no immediate rush. Foster doesn't want a firm answer until the twenty-eighth and you should be back long before then." They heard her flight number being called and Elliott planted a light, affectionate kiss on her lips. "Better hurry now, love, or you'll miss your plane. Ring me from your hotel tonight."

"I will."

Janet gave him one last tentative smile and joined the bustling crowd of holiday-makers who were to share her flight. And once in the air, as she watched the earth fall away, she wondered why she felt such a lack of enthusiasm at Elliott's offer of married life in America. She leaned her head against the seat and closed her eyes. She would think about it later. Right now she had more urgent things to occupy her.

Janet passed the next three hours or so re-reading some of Alison's letters, looking for something — however small — that would give her some kind of clue as to where she might have gone.

The letters were bright and cheerful. There was no question that Alison loved her new job, telling Janet in boundless detail of her life with the children on that small and charming island. She made the work sound easy

14

but Janet knew that it was not. It was no nine to five job looking after twenty or so youngsters, some of them only a few days. Yet, demanding as it must have been, Alison clearly loved it!

She wrote of her daily routine; of the children; of her flat mate, Magdalena, and of how she was helping her to master the difficulties of the Portuguese language. She told Janet of her admiration for Dom Vicente and for his grandson, José Perestrelo. And Janet was quick to sense that whenever the latter's name came up — his attractiveness, his intelligence, his thoughtfulness — Alison's admiration went beyond mere respect for the grandson of her boss. It teetered almost on the brink of hero-worship.

Janet read on, absorbing her sister's account of the Perestrelo's vineyards, sensing that the orphanage was perhaps a sideline for the old, autocratic family, an altruistic gesture to the more unfortunate of the world. She also sensed that perhaps José — more so than the old man — maybe knew something about the sudden appearance of Alison's mysterious boyfriend, and she made a mental note to arrange a meeting with him, too.

At last, when the plane touched down at Funchal airport, Janet stepped out into the soft, sweet air of the Portuguese island of Madeira. The flight had been a good one and, glancing at her watch, Janet found herself wondering how her escort would recognise her, and whether she would have enough time — after booking into her hotel — to enjoy a good lunch before setting out to find Magdalena, and to keep her appointment with Dom Vicente Perestrelo later that afternoon.

2

JANET collected her single suitcase and stood patiently near the exit to the airport, her eyes searching the crowd for the person sent to meet her.

"Miss Robinson?"

A voice from behind made her swing round.

"Yes."

"Allow me," he said, stooping to pick up her suitcase.

The man's tall frame seemed to tower over her as he straightened. He was handsome, there was no denying it, but Janet felt vaguely uncomfortable by the rather bitter set to his mouth.

"I am José Perestrelo," he explained in flawless English. "My grandfather has sent me to meet you." He indicated with his hand. "Please. My car is the blue one over there."

"Thank you. I — I wasn't sure if you'd know who I was, or what time I would be arriving?" She could feel her cheeks reddening as she stammered her reply.

The man's black eyes betrayed some amusement. "This is Madeira, Miss Robinson. It is a small island. Here, we know everything. Besides, it is clear you are not a tourist." He smiled briefly.

"Is it?"

"Very. You are travelling alone. You do not carry the airline's plastic bag containing the customary duty-free wine and you have no companion or family with you. My conclusion? You must be the one who has business with my grandfather, yes?"

Janet laughed. "You'd make a good detective."

Briskly, he picked up her suitcase. "Come. Your reservation is at the hotel Baia Ouro, yes?"

"Yes."

He moved away quickly and Janet

followed. They strode across the airport's crowded concourse towards the car park and, when they reached the blue, open-top car, she left him to see to her case while she climbed into the passenger seat.

Soon they were on the road to Funchal, passing through the steep slopes that tumbled down from the island's lava-clad mountain spine. The roses were out. They were everywhere, climbing along the walls of the tiny houses they passed along the way. Below them lay the glittering ocean while, above them, the sky was blue and clear, and filled with the sound of sea birds as they swooped and dived from the rugged, towering cliffs.

It took around thirty minutes to reach the island's capital and, as they drove through the narrow streets, Janet's eyes darted everywhere. The mosaic pavements glistened in the sun and great tumbling, fragrant masses of bougainvillea seemed to riot over every stone and, away to her right, a broad avenue of trees stretched out towards a magnificent cathedral.

At last, José swung the car into the paved courtyard of the Hotel Baia Ouro and Janet stepped out. He lifted her case from the boot and they mounted the steps of the hotel.

"Just one small bag? With so little luggage you do not intend to stay long on my island?" he observed drily.

Janet smiled, following him up the steps. "I like to travel light but, more seriously, I hope to conclude my business here within a few days."

"Your business with my grand-father?"

"Yes, partly, but there are other things, too."

"Other things?"

"Perhaps you can help me. Can tell me where to find — " She reached into her jacket pocket for her address book and, flipping through it, she read Alison's former address slowly. "The Rua Penha de Franca?"

José Perestrelo threw her a brief,

startled look. "What would interest you there?"

"I'm looking for my sister. Before she went to work at Camacha for your grandfather, she rented an apartment there and made friends with a girl called Magdalena. I thought perhaps she might be able to help me — might know where she is."

His eyes slanted down warily.

"Do you know her?" She thrust the address book under his nose to let him see the girl's almost unpronounceable surname. "Magdalena Lopes Vieira?"

He glanced down and abstractedly corrected her pronunciation before saying in a tone that Janet could not put a name to, "Yes, I have heard of her. If it is the same woman, she is the one who sings in the Taverna Bona Nova." Then he shrugged dismissively. "But perhaps I am mistaken. There are so many Magdalena's in Madeira."

Janet pushed the address book back in her bag. "But you do know my sister, Alison, don't you? She spoke of

21

you in her letters to me."

"Yes, I knew Alison. But, strangely, I did not connect you with her even though I see now how alike you are." The cool, pleasant voice had changed, subtly. "I was under the impression that you were someone more concerned with our wine, a buyer, perhaps. My grandfather did not — "

Knew! Why was he referring to Alison in the past tense?

She asked quickly, "Do you know where my sister might be? Or perhaps you can tell me the name of the man she's supposed to have met and — "

He interrupted abruptly. "I do not know where she is, nor do I know of any man. Alison left our employ very unexpectedly. My grandfather — we liked her. We thought she was settled in her work and we were not only surprised, but we were also very disappointed at the manner and suddenness of her departure." He paused, looking down at her quizzically. "But, then, when one is in love — surely, as her sister, you know all about it?"

"No! No, I don't! That's why I'm here. I've heard nothing from her for five weeks and I want to find out why, or what has happened to her."

"I cannot help you."

He turned away and went through into reception to speak rapidly in Portugese to the man behind the desk. Janet followed him and after a few moments he turned to her, handing her a key.

"My grandfather apologises but, because of business commitments, he will not be able to see you this afternoon after all. But if it is convenient for you, he asks if this evening would be suitable."

"Yes — yes, of course."

"Then I will come back for you at seven o'clock to take you to the Quinta de Montanha Verde."

"Please — Senor Perestrelo — about my sister — "

He straightened, wary again. "Yes?"

"This man she met, surely, you must

know who he is! Can't you tell me anything about him?"

"I know nothing of any man. Come, leave your passport at the desk and I will see you to your room and assist you with your suitcase."

Janet stepped into the lift wondering why she was suddenly getting the feeling that he was holding something back from her.

As they were whisked up to her floor and she leaned against the walnut rail, Janet caught the unique scent of José Perestrelo. Alison was right about one thing at least! In spite of her misgivings, Janet, too, was already finding him to be a very attractive man indeed!

The touch of his arm jerked her back to earth.

"I am sorry if I startled you," he said stiffly. "I was merely letting you know that we have reached your floor."

"Oh — oh, yes!"

As the lift door opened, their eyes met and, disturbingly, she found his gaze lingering over the bright mop of her gold hair. For a moment it looked as though he was about to speak but he didn't. Instead, his hand lightly at her elbow, he led her along a wide, carpeted landing and, when they reached her room, he took the key from her and put it into the door.

Preceding him as he opened it, Janet found herself walking through into a pleasant room with windows opening up on to an old-fashioned, iron balcony.

He placed the suitcase on the stand as she looked around, asking her directly, "Why are you so concerned about the whereabouts of your sister? Why do you feel so strongly that something may have happened to her?"

Somehow, Janet felt the attack in the question — as though he was casting some doubt on her motives for being here.

"I can't say," she answered slowly. "It isn't like her not to write to me for so long. We're very close you see and — "

He strode over to the windows, throwing them open to let in the warm breeze. Then he turned and regarded her sombrely. "Perhaps, Senorita, you are walking into something that does not concern you."

Janet gave a small shudder. "Perhaps, but, all the same, I won't be satisfied until I've found her."

"And how do you intend to do that?"

"I will start by speaking to Magdalena and to your grandfather and then I will go up to Camacha and speak to the matron at the home. Perhaps one of the other nurses knows where she is."

"Have you no-one at home who could help? This is Madeira. It is not the custom for a woman to wander around alone."

Janet nodded, smiling ruefully yet puzzled by his tone. "I don't intend to wander, Senor. And I'm sure I will be quite safe, but I can always telephone my boyfriend if the going gets too much for me. He didn't want me to come here at all. He thinks the same as you — that I'm worrying over nothing."

"If you were my fiancée I would not have given my permission for you to come here alone at all!" He indicated the telephone by the bed. "But, if I can be of assistance — please, let me know."

She nodded again, smiling a little at the rigid chauvinism in his attitude. "Yes, thank you, Senor, I will."

Then his manner changed, becoming suddenly quite equable. "There is no need to call me Senor. As you are to be my grandfather's guest this evening, we can dispense with the formalities and you must call me José. Perhaps, when your business with my grandfather has been concluded, you will join us for dinner. It is unthinkable that you spend you first evening in Madeira alone."

"Thank you, but, no. I couldn't impose — " she began, shaking her head.

"You have made other arrangements?"

"Well, no, not exactly, I — "

"Then I insist!"

He bowed stiffly, reverting to his old, uncompromising manner and then strode away, leaving Janet standing alone in the sunlit room with a faint quiver of alarm running through her. She felt suddenly uneasy. A small voice inside was already confirming her doubts that something was wrong on this beautiful island. And the fragile hope she carried that there might be an easy explanation for her sister's disappearance had suddenly faded because, deep down, she was convinced that José Perestrelo knew more about her sister than he was prepared to admit.

3

JANET threw off her disquieting thoughts and turned her attention to the more uncomplicated task of unpacking her suitcase and, once that was done, she went into the pretty tiled bathroom to shower. Slipping out of her travel-crumpled suit she stood for a few moments in front of the mirror regarding the long, corn-gold hair that framed her oval face. Why had José Perestrelo made her feel so uncomfortable? Or looked at her so oddly? Was it because her appearance was so different from the dark, brown-haired women he had grown up amongst, or was it because she reminded him so much of Alison?

An hour later, lunch over and sitting at one of the tables on the hotel's terrace, Janet glanced around at the straggle of diners still lingering over their meal. She returned the smile from a woman at the next table. The woman leaned across.

"Lovely day, isn't it?"

Janet smiled again. "Yes, lovely."

"I'm Mildred Furnace, and this is my husband, Jack."

Janet introduced herself and then the woman went on, "I was just saying, wasn't I, dear, we haven't seen you here before. Is this your first time in Madeira?" She glanced towards the man who, in turn, nodded politely to Janet.

"Yes, it is."

"I thought so. Jack and I spend most of our time here now that we're retired. We come at least three or four times a year and always stay here at the Baia Ouro. That's how we get to know all of the regulars."

"I see."

"We love it here, don't we, Jack?" Again the man nodded politely as his wife continued. "The weather suits us so well. Take today, for instance, it's perfect for a swim, isn't it?"

Janet murmured her agreement. "Yes, perfect."

Mildred Furness smiled invitingly. "We were wondering, would you care to join us?"

Janet still kept her smile. "Well, that's very kind of you, but no. I'm afraid I can't today. I've promised myself a little sight-seeing."

The woman gave a slight shrug. "Oh, well, never mind — some other time perhaps."

"Yes, perhaps."

Janet picked up her cup and swallowed the rest of her coffee and, as she did so, the woman asked with undisguised curiosity, "Are you here alone?"

A little flustered, Janet answered quickly, "Yes — I mean, not exactly — I'm hoping my sister will join me later."

"I see," the woman said, "then I'm sure you'll both have a lovely time together." Her husband nodded again as the couple rose to their feet and with promises to meet up later, they strolled away.

Strange, Janet thought when they had gone, how normal life seemed to be for everyone. Strange, that while other people were continuing their lives in an ordinary, carefree way, she was locked in inward turmoil, sharing no part of their world while the mystery of her sister's disappearance occupied her thoughts.

* * *

After lunch, the desk clerk supplied Janet with a street map of Funchal and she set off to find the Rua Penha de Franca — and Magdalena. She crossed the square, passing colourful little cafés with their tables spilling out on to the pavements and, resisting the urge to sit at one, she made her way down towards the harbour. Here, the narrow, bustling streets sloped steeply down until they reached the sea. And, as she descended, she threaded her way through them until, at last, she found the Rua Penha de Franca.

Alison's apartment was number twelve and, as Janet pulled on the bell of the main entrance, she could hear the loud, husky tones of a concierge coming from within. A few moments later, the door flew open and a plump, jolly-looking woman of about forty smiled enquiringly and greeted Janet in incomprehensible Portuguese.

Janet, reading from a phrase book, stammered out her reason for being there. "Senora, I am the sister of Alison Robinson. Is Senorita Lopes Vieira at home?"

The concierge beamed, then to Janet's immense relief, her reply came back in a deep, throaty chuckle and in very good English.

"You are Janet?"

"Yes," Janet replied, smiling at the woman's friendly manner.

The concierge made way for her to enter.

"Please, come inside. I am Maria!

33

Your sister has spoken of you many times. How is Alison? Ramondo and me, we miss her. Tell me of her."

Janet stepped into the cool hallway. "I was — I was hoping someone here would tell me of her, Senora. She doesn't seem to be answering my letters and I wondered if perhaps Magdalena could tell me if she's changed her address."

The woman's heavy eyebrows rose. "But Alison is in Camacha."

"No — no, that's just it, Senora, she isn't there now. I — I don't know where she is. Please, can you help me?"

The woman shook her head, bewildered. "She is not here, Senorita Robinson. And if she is not at Camacha, then I do not know where she is."

"Then perhaps Magdalena will be able to help. Is she in?"

The woman frowned and shook her head again. "Magdalena, bah! She thinks she is too good for Ramondo and Maria now! She never comes here!

She stays at the club where she sings for the tourists. Anyway, she cannot help you. They do not speak anymore. She and Alison had — " She paused, frowning distractedly. "I do not know the word in English — "

"A quarrel?"

"Si! Quarrel! They have not spoken to each other for many weeks. Magdalena still pays the rent on the apartment — the money is always put into the bank — but she no longer comes here, except, perhaps to pick up something she needs that has been left here."

Disappointment washed over Janet. She had set out with so much hope and optimism and now, after hearing this, it seemed that she must search elsewhere.

"Thank you, Senora," she murmured softly as she turned away. "I am sorry to take you from your work."

"Senorita!" The concierge called her back, her eyes kind and enquiring. "You are worried, yes?"

"Yes, Senora, I am very worried."

"Then come with me." The woman

held out her arm to Janet. "Come! A suitcase and some of your sister's things are still in the apartment she shared with Magdalena. I have not had any reason to remove them. Her quarrel with the singer did not prevent her from visiting Ramondo and Maria and — when she had some time off from her work — she would come here to stay with us." She shrugged. "Perhaps you will find something to help you — another address, perhaps — amongst her things."

Hope rose again in Janet's heart as she followed Maria up to the next floor. They went along a landing and the woman opened the third door along, inviting Janet in and saying as she opened the shutters, "When you have finished, I will be in my office. I will make coffee, yes? And you must meet my Ramondo."

"Thank you."

The kind eyes regarded Janet. "I hope you find something here to help you."

"Yes, thank you, Senora."

The woman smiled once more and went back to her husband and to her work.

When she had gone Janet looked around. Wine-red curtains draped the balconied window, its glass spattered now with an unexpected shower of rain. A sofa and three leather armchairs were dotted around a single low table in the centre and Janet could see that the apartment was clean and dust-free.

She crossed the room and opened one of the doors to find herself in a small, untidy bedroom. The dressing-table was cluttered with jars and bottles and a couple of dresses were thrown carelessly over the back of a chair. Janet smiled wrily. This room could not be Alison's. Her sister would never tolerate such disarray. Alison was too tidy for words and would often chide Janet for leaving things around.

Janet moved on to the next room. Here, there was not a thing out of place and, as she sat on the edge of her sister's bed, she became aware of the room darkening as the storm passed overhead. Quite suddenly she felt a little lost.

Rising to her feet and with a small touch of guilt, she began her search. She turned the catch of the old-fashioned wardrobe and peered inside to find a number of Alison's jackets and dresses arranged in orderly fashion on their hangers, and several pairs of shoes — Alison's great passion — were aligned neatly above them on a shelf.

"This proves that her going off with someone is nonsense," she murmured to herself as she searched the pockets one by one. "Alison would never leave clothes and shoes behind like this."

Stooping to lift out a suitcase, she opened it up, but, it contained nothing but a couple of folded plastic bags. There was nothing in any of the drawers, either, except for a few handkerchiefs and the odd frilly, sweet-smelling pouch of herbs.

Sighing deeply, Janet sat back on

the bed. This was hopeless! There was nothing here to help her in any way. She glanced down at her hands and sighed wearily again then, after a moment she glanced up, reaching forward to pick up the photograph frame on the bedside table and looking down at the rather squint picture of two golden-haired girls smiling back so happily.

Janet remembered this photograph. It was a good one, taken the last time the sisters had been on holiday together in Scotland. Janet had her own copy at home but, where she had stuck hers out of sight inside an album, Alison's had been enlarged and placed inside this pretty redwood frame.

She gazed thoughtfully down at the laughing face of her sister. "Where are you, Alison?" she murmured, outlining her sister's face with her fingertip. "For goodness' sake, where are you?"

She leaned forward to place the photograph back on to the bedside table, aware of the gentle fragrance of lavender that still clung to her sister's pillow. Then she paused, looking harder at the photograph and wondering what it was that was giving her such an uncomfortable feeling. She picked it up again. Of course! The picture was squint! And fussy, methodical Alison would have had nightmares with such a crooked picture by her bed!

Janet turned the frame over and examined the back. One of the clips had broken off and was causing the picture to slip down between the glass and the backing sheet. She opened it up to straighten it and, as she did so, a thin sheet of pale, blue airmail paper fluttered down on to her lap.

Puzzled, Janet picked it up and unfolded it, reading the words in her sister's familiar, flowery hand. The letter was charged with a kind of urgency and had not been finished and, suddenly, Janet she felt her throat tighten as she read it.

Dear Jan,

I think I've come across something at Camacha that is so awful that it can't possibly be true! I need to talk to someone I can trust. I can't go to the police because I have no proof and they would probably laugh me off the island. And I daren't say a thing to anyone here because I'm not sure yet who's involved. Besides, I may have made an almighty mistake. I do hope so. I need you, my dear, logical little sister to tell me that I'm imagining things again, just like you used to when we were children. Remember how good you were at solving my little mysteries? Remember the time you cracked the case of 'The Missing Ballet Shoe'? But this is no game, Jan, and I have to do SOMETHING. Please, Jan, phone me soon. I have to confide in someone or I'll go crazy —

There the letter ended abruptly and Janet glanced quickly at the date. It had

41

been written just over five weeks ago!

She sat bolt upright and, with shaking hands, put the frame together again. Then, as though frozen to the bed, she read the letter twice more before thrusting it into her jacket pocket and getting to her feet.

This was incredible! What had Alison discovered at Camacha that had alarmed her so? And who was the someone — or something — that had not only interrupted her, but had clearly alerted her to the danger of her knowledge being discovered? So much so, that she had had the forethought to hide it inside the photo frame thinking it would be safe there until she could finish it later?

But Alison never had finished it! And it was pure good fortune that Janet had found it and, for the first time in her life, Janet was thankful for her sister's fastidious ways.

Frowning deeply, she turned her head towards the window as though looking for inspiration. She found none but knew that her instincts had been right all along! Alison was in trouble!

Back in her room at the Hotel Baia Ouro, Janet curled up on the bed still deep in thought. What must she do? If she told anyone about the note she could place her sister in even more danger! She shivered, suddenly feeling cold. The sun had moved towards the west, filling the room with a golden wash of colour and, glancing at her watch, she realised she would have to hurry if she was to be ready for José Perestrelo when he called for her at seven.

4

ON the stroke of seven the man from reception rang through to tell her that the Senor was waiting for her downstairs. And, still numb with shock at the contents of Alison's letter, Janet went down to meet him.

With the minimum of greeting, José drove her to his home through the labyrinth of steeply-rising cobbled streets and up on to the mountain road. They spoke only of the island and of its beauty, and Janet was glad in a way as she tried to clear her head by breathing in the warm, perfume-laden air that wafted in through the open windows of his car.

She gazed out thoughtfully. Madeira, island of flowers. Precious jewel of the Atlantic and everything that Alison had said it was! But as Janet glanced up at the mountains, their peaks now collared with evening cloud, she knew she must find her sister before succumbing to its spell.

José made a sudden turn into a curving driveway and, at last, Janet caught her first glimpse of the red-tiled, turreted roof of the Perestrelo's home, Quinta de Monthana Verde. Portuguese style, and well-lit by the lights from the courtyard, the casa stood in grounds of carefully-watered lawns, its green shutters folded back against its white walls. And although she couldn't see them in the evening's shadow, she pictured the vineyards that surrounded it, sweeping away in steep grey ribbons of lava setts.

"Welcome to my home."

José held the car door for Janet to step out and already a man was hurrying down the steps to greet them.

"Senor José! Senorita!"

"This is Pedro, our manager — and our right-hand man," José explained. "He takes care of our vineyards but his responsibilities go much further than that. Is that not so, Pedro?"

"Si, Senor," the man replied. "I am a man of many parts but it is no matter." He gave a small bow. "It is a delight to meet you, Senorita Robinson."

Janet smiled as the manager shook her hand, a little surprised that he was already familiar with her name. Then, saying something in Portuguese to José and saluting her once more, Pedro strode briskly away around the back of the house.

Janet, following José, climbed the sweeping flight of marble steps that led up to the house. At the top, a wide, ornate door opened and, leaning heavily on an ebony stick, an older man appeared.

Silver-haired and dignified, the aristocratic Dom Vicente Perestrelo shook her hand, saying sombrely in the same flawless English as his son, "Senorita, it is always a happy day for me when I have the honour to greet a guest from England."

46

"It is a happy day for me also, Dom Vicente," Janet replied quietly. "And I am very grateful that you are giving me the opportunity to talk to you of my sister."

He gave a dry, little smile as he led her along a wide corridor and into a cool, exquisitely-furnished room.

"Later — first we must take refreshment. Allow me to offer you dinner."

As she turned to follow him, she felt José's hand touch her elbow. It was only a touch but it had the power to make her throat contract, and already it was sending shivers down her spine. Never had a mere touch played upon her senses like this! He was powerful, attractive and dangerous. And he was scaring her silly! She gave herself a mental shake. This was no time for thoughts such as these! She was here on serious business, not to wilt at the sensual touch of a good-looking stranger.

As though sensing her reaction,

he glanced down, his gaze lingering quizzically over her bright mop of hair, then his hand tightened a little more around her arm as he led her through into the dining-room.

The room was bathed in the light of a dozen candles. They glinted on the silver and the crystal, and on the fine white linen of the cloth. And, as they ate, Janet pondered whether the Perestrelo's had ever shown her sister such hospitality and, more dangerously, whether it was the effect of the wine that was affecting her senses whenever she looked José's way.

"This is excellent wine, Dom Vicente," she commented in an attempt to ease her tension.

Dom Vicente inclined his head in response to her compliment. "This wine is older than I am, Senorita." He smiled. "And I believe it is in far better condition."

"Perhaps, Janet," José observed drily, "we humans should be more like the wines of Madeira. With each generation something new is added, a rare flavour that keeps it forever young. This wine we drink tonight is one of my great-grandfather's first bottles. I hope someday that my great-grandson will say the same and find a little of it in me."

"In one respect, you are lacking in that," Dom Vicente rebuked.

"Which respect is that, Grandfather?"

"When my father was your age, he already had three strong sons." And, as José's eyes slid to Janet's, he added acidly, "I trust you will shortly remedy that state of affairs."

For some unaccountable reason, Janet found herself growing hot, but José gave an easy smile.

"I hope to do just that, Grandfather. And perhaps sooner than we know." He glanced again at Janet with a challenging glint in the depths of his dark eyes.

Janet felt desperate. She decided right then that the time was long overdue to make crystal clear the real purpose of her visit to Madeira.

"Senor Dom Vicente, about my sister — "

But he put up a restraining hand. "Not here, little one — "

Later, when dinner was over and they had withdrawn to an anteroom, a woman brought coffee, placing it on a low table beside an open, log fire. Heavy curtains had been drawn across the windows and chandeliers blazed.

It was only when the woman had left and Janet sipped on the sweet, dark coffee that the opportunity arose to ask again of her sister.

"Dom Vicente, please, I need news about my sister."

The old man shook his head and held up his hand. He said nothing, remaining silent for many long moments — so long, in fact, that Janet wondered if he'd forgotten she was there at all. It happened sometimes when age took its toll. And, as she waited, she watched the changing expressions flicker across the lined, aristocratic face.

At last he stirred, his shrewd dark eyes probing her face before saying softly, "Your sister has left our employ. As I told you when you telephoned, we received, at very short notice, a note that said she could not come to Camacha again because she was going away to marry someone. That is over five weeks ago and she has not been seen at Camacha since." He shook his head. "One does not leave one's employer like that. It is bad practice, no?"

"But — my sister would not act so irresponsibly! There is clearly a reason that caused her to leave in that way! And that reason is what I wish to find out. Surely, in the time she was with you, you would have learned of her integrity, of her conscientiousness?"

"Yes, we thought we knew her well, and her leaving in such a manner distressed us. But — " He spread his hands. "It seems she met some people — new friends — and no doubt lost her heart to one of them.

When one is young, love can be a strange mistress. She can force one's personality to change drastically and make even the most sensible of us to act out of character."

Janet felt caught somewhere between fear and hope. Fear for her sister and the tiny, glimmering hope that she had been given another slender lead.

"These people she met, Dom Vicente," she urged, "who are they? Where can I find them?"

He shrugged his thin shoulders. "If I knew that I would tell you, child, but I know nothing more. As it is — " He shrugged again and pressed a despairing hand to his forehead.

"Please," she begged, her voice so quiet it was almost inaudible, "you must know something about them! You must help me, Dom Vicente!"

"I do not know that I can."

José Perestrelo had been standing a little apart but now he stepped forward, his tone icy cold. "Your sister had a contract. It is not the custom here to break a contract without good reason. And I, for one, do not consider falling in love a good enough reason!"

Janet looked at him briefly, replying through tight lips, "My sister would not renege on her contract if that is what you're implying. If it has been broken then, as I've already pointed out, it must have been for a very good reason — "

José's grandfather raised a hand in mild rebuke.

"José! José, Senorita Robinson is our guest. I will not allow you to use such a tone with her."

José excused himself, throwing her a look of cold indifference before retreating once more to the back of the room.

Janet turned back to the old man to ask stiffly, "May I have your permission to visit your children's home at Camacha tomorrow, Dom Vicente?"

"Certainly, but if you are hoping to learn more of your sister there, please do not build up your hopes too much. When Alison's note arrived I sent Pedro to persuade her to change her mind — to complete her contract if only for the sake of the children. He could not find her. Her room at the home had been cleared of her belongings and the ones who knew her — her colleagues — all said the same thing. That she had met a man and gone away."

"All the same," Janet said quietly, "I would still like to go. Perhaps they have heard something more since then."

"Of course," the old man agreed kindly, patting her hand, "you must do all you can to allay your worries. But, to reach Camacha you must cross the mountains and I beg you to be careful. It is a remote area and it can be dangerous to someone who does not understand the terrain. I suggest you hire a car or, better still, take a taxi. You must have someone with you who knows the way."

"There is no need for any of that."

José's clipped voice came once more from behind. "I will escort the Senorita to Camacha."

Janet turned her head to look at him. "That's very kind of you, but I'm sure I'll manage perfectly well — "

"Let me be the judge of that," he said. "As my grandfather says, the mountains can be treacherous to a stranger."

"That is an excellent suggestion, José," Dom Vicente agreed, nodding his head. "And, while you are there, you must see why our Camacha vineyard has not yet completed the quota."

"Yes, Grandfather. That was also my intention." José glanced anxiously at the old man who was now pressing his fingertips against his eyes. His manner puzzled Janet as his mood switched now to a business-like abruptness. He reached across for her jacket, holding it for her and clearly indicating that the interview was at an end.

"Please, my grandfather can tell you nothing more of your sister," he muttered, "and he has been far from well. Tomorrow I will telephone your hotel to let you know what time we will leave for Camacha. It is a long drive so please be ready when I call."

Janet was suddenly very tired. The early flight and the emotional time at Alison's flat had drained her more than she realised. Her body felt heavy with fatigue and her mind was growing numb.

"Being late is not one of my habits," she retorted wearily.

"Then I will see you in the morning."

He raised his hand in salute and left the room, closing the door firmly behind him.

Dom Vicente smiled and shook his head. "My grandson's manner is somewhat imperious, yes? But you must not judge him by that, Senorita Janet. He has many pressures upon him and the fact that he has a guest — an old friend — staying here with us, seems to be adding to them."

The old man smiled a little wearily.

"But I should not trouble you with our affairs. You have enough of your own. Come, Pedro will take you back to your hotel. Perhaps tomorrow will bring good news of your sister."

Back in her room, and when Pedro had long since returned to the Casa de Monthana Verde, Janet stepped out on to the veranda to stand beneath the black velvet of the sky. It was still warm, and the air was heavily-scented as she breathed it in. She felt a little dreamy, no doubt brought on by the unaccustomed amount of wine she had drunk over dinner or was it the dangerous discovery of the way José Perestrelo affected her? Surely, he must have sensed how he'd made her feel?

Janet swivelled suddenly. This was crazy thinking! And, thrusting all thoughts of the good-looking Madeiran out of her head, she crossed the room and picked up the phone to dial Elliott's number.

5

THE next morning, a little after nine thirty, José Perestrelo picked Janet up from her hotel and they set off for the orphanage that lay beyond Camacha. It was already too humid and she drooped in her seat, looking out over the plantations of bananas and sugar cane, and at the straw-topped shelters that shaded the fat, sleepy-looking cattle.

And, as they drove, she listened to José's attractive voice giving her a kind of travelogue, suggesting — after an hour — that they stop at the next village for coffee.

"I could do with something long and cool, thanks," Janet agreed.

"Of course."

Ten minutes later, José swung off the road into what turned out to be no more than a huddle of houses clustering around a tiny square, and with a small, inviting bar as its focal point. It was high up in the mountains and thankfully, as Janet stepped out of the car, the air felt cooler on her face.

José led her to a single trestle table by the bar's open door, still continuing with his travelogue and telling her of the famous explorers who had discovered his land.

When the woman came to take their order he asked for lemonade and, while they waited, his eyes drifted to Janet's ringless hand.

"This man you spoke of — " he asked curiously. "The man in England — "

"Who? Elliott?"

"Yes, Elliott. He is to be your husband?"

Janet gave him a surprised look. She hadn't expected that. "My husband? No. Well, yes — I suppose so."

"No? Yes? Suppose?" A dark eyebrow lifted. "Well, is he or isn't he?"

"I honestly don't know." She shrugged

slightly. "Probably."

"But you are not sure?"

The woman came back with their lemonade and, as she set the glasses down, Janet turned her head away from his dark, laser eyes.

"Of course, I'm sure," she answered, when the woman had gone again. "It's just that — well, we have things to consider."

"Do you love him?"

"You surely don't expect me to answer that?"

José laughed softly. "Why not? It is a simple enough question."

"I'm afraid it's none of your business."

He laughed again, even more softly. "Then you do not love him, that is clear enough."

"Don't be ridiculous." She took a long, cool drink, finishing the lemonade in a single refreshing quaff then, putting the glass down with a jolt, she added sharply, "Hadn't we better be making a move?"

"Presently. First I wish to show you

something." He stood up and held out his hand. "Come."

Janet took hold of his hand and walked with him along a narrow path that straddled the steep slopes of the mountainous terrain. They were now in the heart of Madeira and it was some little time before she realised that she was standing on the outer rim of the island's volcanic core.

They stopped by the rail-protected edge to look down into the crater that lay two thousand feet below, and at the tiny village nestling in its shadows.

"What is that place?" she asked.

"It is the Curral das Freiras — the Corral of the Nuns," he explained.

"A convent?"

"Yes, but it is not only that."

"Do other people live there?"

"Yes." He glanced at her with a crooked smile. "It is a good place to live, yes?"

"But it's so remote — so hidden away — "

"That is the reason the convent was

built there in the first place."

"What do you mean?"

"Long ago, when the pirates came to Madeira, the men would hide their women and children in the corral to keep them from harm."

"From rape and pillage?"

"Something like that."

"But who would want to live in such an inaccessible place nowadays?"

José laughed. "There's something to be said for opting out of this frenzied world, don't you think?"

Janet nodded. "Mmm, I suppose there is." She gazed down on the miniature village lying below them so peacefully. "It certainly looks tranquil enough."

She felt the light touch of his arm come around her shoulder as he said, "Once, when no outsiders could reach it, it was said that a man could live there for a hundred years and never grow old. Now, of course, it is different. Since they built the road, it is usually swamped with tourists."

Janet looked down reflectively. "It would be wonderful to live in such a quiet, contented way, wouldn't it?"

José laughed again, more bitterly this time. "It is no Shangri-La. Come, now that you have seen one of our main tourist attractions, we must be on our way."

Janet turned away from the crater's edge with a slight feeling of dizziness and, when the warmth of José's hand came once more into her own, she knew it wasn't only the height that was bringing on the feeling.

They continued on towards Camacha and, as he drove, she listened again as he explained to her now of the cultivation of the Perestrelo wine. He told her of how the plots were terraced, and of how they were worked by the descendants of the families who had been loyal to the Perestrelos for generations. And he told her, too, of the way mules were still used to cart the vintage to town because no-one had yet discovered a method to better it.

"Look!" he said, pointing up at the mountain. "Beyond that village lies Camacha! From here, we must continue our journey by foot."

Janet looked upwards towards the summit, asking in astonishment, "Can't we keep to the road?"

"We could, but my way is more interesting." He threw her a grin, filled with mischievous amusement. "Do you think you can make it?"

"Of course I can!" she answered, resenting the fact that he seemed to think she couldn't.

"Then let's go."

He parked the car on a verge and they began their climb, following a watercourse, just one of the many that irrigated the terraces below. A little over an hour later, they finally reached the village.

On that mellow morning, everyone was working on the vintage. Men, women, and children, too, were busy filling up the funnel-shaped baskets with grapes ready to be taken to the press. And, as Janet watched them, fascinated, José explained how the villagers still trod on the grapes, turning them into the purple liquid of wine.

Once pressed, it would later be poured into goatskin pouchers — some of which held ten gallons or more — ready to be slung on to their shoulders to go to a collection point and be taken farther down the mountain by mule to where the trucks waited to transport them to Funchal.

The orphanage was several miles farther up the mountain and Janet felt a stab of dismay when José told her he must conclude his business with the wine first before he could take her up there. So, hot and tired, as he disappeared into the shadow of a doorway, she waited for him in the shade of a eucalyptus tree, seating herself on a log that lay abandoned at its base.

A village woman came out to her with bread rolls and some cheese, and a small pitcher of cool, white wine to quench her thirst. When José rejoined her a little while later he seemed irritated and impatient, telling her briskly that none of his grape-pickers had heard any more news of Alison.

They eventually set off again, following the same water course for a couple miles more. They were up on the high slopes of the mountain now, surrounded by wild countryside and picking their careful way along the narrow path. And, as she looked down on to the valleys below, the knowledge that there was nothing more than a six-foot verge as leeway was enough to test even the bravest heart.

Suddenly, they came to a place where the watercourse cut into a sheer, vertical rock and José turned to her to ask gently, "Do you think you can manage this?"

Janet gaped at him in disbelief. Surely he wasn't suggesting that they take the path around the rock? It was fairly wide — a good five feet across — but there was nothing to save them should they take a false step.

Her eyes widened in alarm. "You're kidding me, aren't you?"

He shook his head. "No. I do not make joke."

"But I can't. I can't walk on that!"

"There is no other way, Janet."

"But there must be! This path is bad enough. I'm terrified of heights — I can't possibly — "

"Then I will carry you across."

Janet's eyes widened even more. "Carry me?"

"Don't be afraid. I shall carry you on my shoulders, as I've often carried the grapes."

Her legs turned to jelly as he stooped, instructing her to sit piggy-back style on his shoulders.

"No, José. No, it's all right — I'll manage."

"Come, I will feel better knowing I have you safely on my back. It will be quicker this way."

Hardly able to speak, somehow she straddled herself across his broad back, closing her eyes and hanging on for all she was worth.

"Don't worry," he said brightly as he strode forward, "I've carried more than your weight before today."

Her teeth chattered. "José, please — "

"Stay quite still. Pretend you're a goatskin and don't move."

She closed her eyes tightly, not even daring to take a breath as he made his way along the path. His powerful muscles bore her along until, after what seemed a lifetime, they reached the other side and he finally put her down.

"There!" he said. "That wasn't too bad, was it?"

Janet looked up at him, her legs still trembling and her lips quivering. "That was awful!"

His eyes moved over her pale, stricken face, concern filling his eyes. "Were you so afraid."

"Of course, I was," she muttered. "I was scared stiff."

"Then come." He took hold of her hand, squeezing it a little and trying to make light of her ordeal. "Let us rest a while. Look, here is a good place."

He pulled her down on to a soft bed of herbs, smiling now and stroking her cheek with a long stem of grass. It tickled, and, in spite of her fraught nerves, it made her laugh.

"Please — don't ever ask me to play a goatskin again," she told him firmly. "Once is enough for anyone!"

He grinned down at her, his dark eyes filled with mischievous amusement. "We still have to come back."

Janet snorted. "Not that way! We'll go back by road. We'll hitch a lift if we have to."

Still grinning, he put his strong, brown arm around her narrow waist. "I rather enjoyed it."

"Well, I didn't!"

She looked up into his face, suddenly aware of his tall, muscular body so very close to her own. His arm came around her shoulders and she felt his hand gently massaging the nape of her neck. When he spoke, his voice was soft, tender, murmuring against her cheek, "How tense you are."

Suddenly, he was kissing her and, in that one moment, all danger was forgotten. Janet felt his arms lock more intimately around her and despite her fear, she made no protest as his mouth came down upon her own.

José held her in a long, sweet kiss; not brutal or hard, but full of tenderness and gentleness.

Janet couldn't move, nor did she want to. She knew she had made no mistake about the depth of her feelings for this man, and she knew, too, that he was assessing her, absorbing every quivering reaction to his touch.

He raised his head, speaking softly, his tone full of conviction. "I could make you forget your lover in England."

Janet glanced up quickly, twisting herself out of his embrace, "José . . . "

He drew back a little, his eyes subdued in the shadow. "I know you feel as I do. This is real — "

"Real?" Her voice rose as she tried to resist the truth of his words. "How can it be real when we hardly know each other?"

"But I do know. We both know, don't we? It is in our chemistry, no?"

Panic drove her to her feet, dashing his arms away and horrified to find how strongly she was attracted to this man.

"Please — José — " she stammered. "I'm here to find my sister, not to — " She broke off, completely out of her depth and taking a few faltering steps forward. "Let's go. Physical chemistry is natural between a man and a woman so let's not encourage it. I've no time for games of this sort."

"Games? Is that how you see it? A game?"

"It can be nothing else."

He stood up and came to her side, frowning a little and caressing her cheek with the side of his index finger. "It is no game we play, and you know it. Can't you feel it? Couldn't you feel it the moment we met at Funchal airport?"

Janet put up a hand as if to ward him off but he took hold of it, turning the palm upward and bending his dark head to it, kissing it before he said sombrely, "You will learn, my pretty one. One day I will teach you of love but, yes, first we must find your sister. Come."

José's dark mood lifted as they continued on their way, walking ever upwards along the toe-bruising path, and passing waterfalls that cascaded from the sheer, grey-white cliffs.

At last, when almost an hour had passed, he paused, looking upwards and pointing into the trees.

"Look!" he exclaimed. "The orphanage."

Janet squinted up, too, and felt a comforting sense of relief as the building came into view. It was a long, single-storeyed house, almost obscured by the impenetrable scrub pine around it and with only the sound of goats' bells to break the silence.

It took a few minutes to reach it and, as they went through the doorway, it took a few more before Janet's eyes became accustomed to the gloom. A woman was waiting in the shadows, fiftyish, dark-haired and wearing the blue, starched dress of a matron.

6

THE woman rose, stepping forward with an outstretched hand. "Senor José, welcome," she said before turning to Janet with open curiosity.

"Senora Matrona," José replied, murmuring his greetings in Portuguese before continuing in English. "This is Janet, the sister of Alison. She has come a long way for news of her."

The matron shook Janet's hand with a hard, mannish grip, and there was an almost frozen efficiency about her style.

"You must be exhausted, Miss Robinson. Please, both of you, come into my office and allow me to offer you refreshment."

Janet made to follow, relishing the thought of a drink and a rest, but paused, turning back when José remained where he was in the dark hallway.

"Senora Matrona," he said, "they told me in Camacha that Pedro had come up to the orphanage. Is he still here?"

The woman stared, surprise showing in her eyes. "Pedro? No. He was here some time ago to pick up some papers but he left for Funchal over an hour ago."

José cursed softly. "Do you know which papers he took away?"

"No, I do not."

"Then I shall have to check in the reception office myself. Will you excuse me, Janet? I'm sure you can ask the matrona about Alison without my help."

Janet gave a small shrug. "OK."

When he went outside, the matron led Janet through into her office and invited her to sit in a plastic chair by the desk. A tray of iced tea was already waiting and the woman handed her a glass. Then she settled back in a swivel chair and regarded Janet speculatively.

"Now, Senorita Janet, how may I

help?" she asked.

Janet began to ask the now-familiar questions about her sister's whereabouts, her heart growing heavier as she watched the woman shake her head.

"I know nothing. The day Alison left, I was in Funchal. When I came back here, she had already gone. Look, here is the note she left."

She opened a drawer in the desk and handed Janet a single page. It was in Alison's handwriting, there was no question about that. It simply said that she had met someone and was leaving to go to him, and that she would write later to explain more fully.

Janet looked across at the matron, her face pale. "May I keep this?"

"Of course."

"Senora, everyone talks of this man but, so far, no-one has given me a name. Do you know who he is, or where I can find him? Can you tell me anything about him?"

"I know nothing."

"Then perhaps one of the other

members of your staff?"

"No, they know nothing either. We went through all this with Pedro when Alison first went away."

"Then perhaps one of the children?"

The matron sighed. "The children know even less. You realise that when they come here they already know the pain of losing a dear one. We make it a rule that when any of the staff has reason to leave, we break the news very gently to the children, very gently. You understand?"

Janet stared down at the glass of iced tea, not at all happy with the woman's negative response. "Yes, I can understand that. But surely, there must be someone who can tell me something."

As Janet looked back at the woman she could see that she no longer held her attention. The matron had looked away towards the window, her body still and her hands clenched. Then she suddenly jerked her head back to Janet, staring at her a little wildly.

"Please, Senorita, I can tell you nothing more. Your sister has gone away with some man and that is all I know. Now you must excuse me, I have much to do. The children will be back soon and I must prepare. Please — enjoy your tea."

The woman stood up abruptly, spilling a holder of pencils in her rush to leave the room and leaving Janet alone in the office, bewildered and uneasy. Something had evidently unnerved the woman and Janet got up to look out of the window, but she could see nothing, except a car driving away. A few minutes later, she heard footsteps coming towards the door.

"Well," José said as he came into the office, "was the matrona able to help you?"

"No, she wasn't. And what's more, I'm even more convinced that something weird is going on."

"What do you mean? And where is the matrona?" he demanded.

"You tell me!" Janet flung her arm

around, indicating vaguely towards the window. "She saw something out there and just flew out."

"But why? What did she see?"

Exasperated, Janet shrugged, accusation in her tone and her eyes troubled. "I don't know! But she saw something, I'm sure of it, because the next thing she did was to leap up and run out as if her life depended on it." Her voice took on a shriller note. "She — she — "

"OK, calm down." He put his hands on her shoulders to steady her and asked quietly, "Now, tell me exactly what happened."

Janet told him again of the matron's odd reaction when she looked out of the window, and then of her hurried departure, but before she finished, José had already strode to the door and out into the hallway. He returned after a few minutes shaking his head.

"Her car has gone," he told her, his eyes narrow. "There is no sign of her."

Janet sighed. "I know."

José was frowning deeply, saying, almost to himself, "Something must have spooked her. But I saw nothing out there — "

"What on earth is going on here, José?" Janet asked warily. "And, if this is a children's home, where are all the children? And where is the staff?"

He shook his head, only half-listening as he answered vaguely, "The children are in Camacha."

"Camacha? Why?"

"They go to school there, and the staff go with them. They are the teachers."

"But what about the babies? Surely there is someone here to look after them?"

He gave her a puzzled look. "The babies? There are no babies here. All the children are at school."

"That's not true. Alison wrote often of the babies."

He shook his head again. "There have never been babies here. You must be mistaken."

80

She fell silent, her eyes staring and a terrible blank look coming over her face.

"I am not mistaken. My sister spoke of babies," she said in a whisper, her voice barely audible.

"OK," he said, after a long pause, "if you say so."

"I do say so!"

He regarded her for a long time, as though analysing her words in his head. Then he said briskly, "Come, let us go back to Funchal. Our business is finished here for today. I will telephone the matrona tonight and arrange to come back tomorrow to talk to the staff about your sister."

"Can't we talk to them now? On our way back through Camacha?"

"No. I must speak with the matrona first."

Janet shrugged, unsure of his logic. "Well, if you say so. But there's no way I'm going back the way we came."

"You don't have to. I've borrowed one of the trucks to take us back."

They went outside and José helped her into a dusty, old truck. And, as they drove away, Janet frowned. What kind of a children's home was it where there was no sign of children — no sign of a ball or a doll?

She felt cold. Even as the warm, pine-scented breeze sang against her cheek, Janet sat shivering on a rising hysteria of hopelessness. Beside her, José drove on, silent and as taut as a wire. Then, suddenly, and without restraint, Janet started to weep — it was the measure of her tiredness.

The truck's speed slowed as José pulled over and braked. Warm and strong, his arm slid round her and Janet leaned back to rest her head against his shoulder.

"Do not be afraid, cara," he murmured, his handsome face against her hair. "You are tired, and when we are tired our imagination begins to play tricks. Tonight you must rest and tomorrow I will come for you again and, together, we will find more news of Alison."

He held her close, and Janet clung on to him for dear life, listening to his gentle words of comfort.

★ ★ ★

Back at her hotel and when José had finally left her alone in her room, Janet lay down on the bed. Memories of her sister surfaced and twisted through her mind, making sleep impossible as she tried to make some sense of it. But she could find no sense. All she could think of was Alison . . . and José . . .

José. Even the very thought of him sent waves running through her like an electric shock. She could hear his voice, feel his touch — she must stop this!

She reached out abruptly, switching on the bed-side lamp as she picked up the phone. Elliott — she must speak to Elliott. He would bring some sense into her life again — some normality. And he would come to Madeira to help her. Help her look for Alison. Help her to fight off her feelings for José.

She knew he would be at home. He was a precise man and he hated to stray even a little from his steady, comfortable routine. She dialled the number and lay back against the pillows as his phone rang out. Then there was a click and Elliott's sleep-heavy voice came down the line.

"Hanson."

"Elliott? It's me, Janet."

"Janet! Do you know what time it is?"

She glanced down at her wrist and checked the time. It was a little after two in the morning in England.

"I'm sorry, Elliott. I had no idea it was so late. Have I woken you?"

"It doesn't matter," he mumbled tiredly, adding as an afterthought, "Is something up?"

"I don't really know, Elliott," she began uncertainly.

"What is it? Are you ill?"

"No, I'm — I'm OK, it's just that — oh, it's nothing really. I just needed to talk to you."

"What about?"

"Anything . . . nothing . . . "

She broke off. What was the matter with her?

"Nothing? You've woken me up at this hour just to tell me you feel like talking about nothing?"

She heard a tinge of irritation creeping into Elliott's tone.

"Look, love," he went on more patiently, "I'm sorry you're on edge but, if you're not ill, will you get on with why you're ringing me this late? There must be something. Is it to do with Alison?"

"Yes," she answered flatly.

"Still no news?"

"No, I'm afraid not."

"Has this Perestrelo chap been of any help?"

"Ahh — well — Elliott — "

"What is it? You sound funny."

"Do I? It's — it's nothing."

She rubbed her fingers along her brow, smoothing over the worried line before taking a deep, sighing breath.

"Elliott, I need you here. Can you get away?"

"Probably, in a couple of days," he said matter-of-factly.

"That's no use. I meant, can you come now? Tomorrow?"

"Tomorrow? Are you kidding?"

"No, I'm not kidding. I'm getting desperate. Every lead I get hold of turns out to be a wild-goose chase."

"But you've only been there a couple of days. Give it time."

"Please, Elliott! Please come! I need you here!"

"Hey, steady on, no need to get into a panic. Like I said, Alison probably wouldn't like the idea of you sticking your nose into her business anyway."

"No, you're wrong. I've found a note."

"A note? From Alison?"

"Yes."

"Well, there you are then. I told you she'd probably forgotten to post it off."

"No, you've got it wrong. She

86

didn't send it to me — I found it by accident."

"Where?"

"In her room."

"And that's a problem?"

"Yes, it is."

"What does it say?"

"That's just it, I — I can't tell you over the phone. That's why I want you here."

She heard his deep sigh, then, "Look, Jan, I have a few problems, too."

"What problems?" she asked, a worried quiver coming into her voice.

"I'm seeing Foster about the American job tomorrow and I can't get away just now. Perhaps in a couple of days — "

Her hand gripped more fiercely around the handset as memories of José's touch burned against her face. "A couple of days may be too late!"

She heard his impatient sigh come down the wire. "Too late? What the heck is wrong with you, Janet? You're making this problem with your sister sound as though it's the end of the world."

"Don't make jokes, Elliott. I'm serious. Please come over," she begged, her voice becoming shrill.

"I can't, Jan. At least, not right now. Give me a couple of days and for now, let me get back to sleep. You, too. Everything will seem different in the morning. Try to calm down and we'll talk tomorrow. 'Bye, love — "

"Elliott! No! Don't ring off yet! Forget your meeting tomorrow and come over to me. I need you here!"

He gave another deep, impatient sigh. "Look, I can't just drop everything and rush off to Madeira! I've told you, Alison will turn up so why don't you stop this worrying? You ought to know that without me having to spell it out for you. My meeting tomorrow is about that American job and you know how important it is to me. Important to both of us if you decide to come. And I'll try to come over in a couple of days, OK?"

"Elliott — " She began to protest but his voice cut across sounding more impatient.

"Don't be so dramatic, darling, it's not like you."

He paused, and then he went on, his manner becoming soothing, "Look, I'll ring you tomorrow, OK? Now get some sleep and don't worry. Alison will be fine, you'll see."

She heard the click as the line went dead.

Janet lay back against the pillow, the phone dangling loosely in her hand as she stared up at the ceiling. And from somewhere deep inside came a feeling of inevitability . . .

7

THERE was a wild storm in the night. The wind howled and screamed around the walls of the hotel, rattling the windows and shutters until Janet felt that they would be blown out into the ocean by the strength of it.

She lay curled up in bed, tucking her head below the sheets in an effort to shut it away but, knowing, too, that even if the storm had not blown up, and in spite of her fatigue, sleep would never have come to her tonight.

She rose to a dull, sunless day, her nerves at breaking point as she rang room service for coffee. A little after eight thirty, the telephone rang, its sound reminding her with a jolt of Elliott — he was probably phoning to apologise for his impatience with her last night.

However, when she answered it wasn't Elliott. Instead, the deep, attractive voice of José Perestrelo came down the line.

"Will you be ready by ten o'clock if I come for you then?"

"Yes," she replied, her heart lifting, "I'll be ready."

Almost as soon as she'd replaced the receiver she heard a soft tap on the door. She went to open it.

"Senorita Robinson?"

Janet regarded the beautiful young woman standing there. "Yes?"

"I am Magdalena Lopes Vieira. I wish to speak to you. May I enter?"

Janet stepped back in stunned surprise. "Why — yes — please do."

Magdalena swept past Janet and walked into the centre of the room, her movements graceful and her sensuous hips swaying. Her coal-black hair hung loose and heavy, swinging across her shoulders, and her face, as she turned back to Janet, was heart-shaped and with high cheekbones.

91

"I speak on the telephone to Maria last night," she said, her voice husky and filled with elusive undertones. "She told me you have been to my apartment asking for news of your sister."

Janet indicated for Magdalena to be seated, but the lovely girl demurred, choosing to remain where she was in the centre of the room.

"Yes — yes, I was there," she admitted. "I wanted to know if you had any idea where Alison had got to. I haven't heard from her, you see, and as you are her friend, I thought, perhaps, you might know where she is."

"I was her friend, but I am no longer." The girl's dark, almond-shaped eyes glittered like jet and her small chin rose haughtily. "I am told she left the orphanage to go off with a man." She paused, frowning a little before continuing a trace of uncertainty creeping into her husky voice. "That is so, is it not?"

"That's what people are saying. Do you know if it is true?"

"Perhaps." Magdalena gave a deep sigh. "But, perhaps not. I cannot see into Alison's heart."

"But you must know something. Why else would you wish to see me?"

"Perhaps I know something," the girl repeated vaguely, "and then again, perhaps not."

"Senorita Vieira," Janet went on, already beginning to feel a little exasperated at the girl's evasiveness, "what can you tell me? What is it that brought you here today?"

Magdalena gave a small shrug, turning her face to the view outside the window. The movement was graceful and even in her increasingly belligerent mood Janet couldn't deny the outstanding beauty of the Madeiran girl.

"I come because Maria thinks I may be able to help you and because I may have once seen the man."

Janet looked long and hard at Magdalena. "Please, Senorita, please continue. I'm desperate for news."

"But I could be mistaken. Perhaps

it is not the same man." The girl shrugged. "But I can tell you of a place that Alison spoke of — she may have gone there."

"And where is that?"

"I hear her once — speaking to someone on the telephone — ask the way to Cabo Girao."

"Cabo Girao?" Janet repeated slowly.

"Yes. It is a — how you call it — a village. But why Alison should wish to go there I do not know! It is very high in the mountains. And there is nothing to do there except sit under the trees and watch the goats."

Janet made a mental note of the name as Magdalena went on. "I think the man she spoke to on the telephone is the man she brought into the club."

"Club?"

"Yes. Where I sing. I think he is an Englishman, or maybe, an American — "

"Did you meet him? Do you know who he is?"

Magdalena shook her head gracefully.

"No. I was on the stage, singing, but I saw her sitting with him at a table, sitting close, like lovers. And later, after my show, she brought him to my dressing-room, but I — I had not the time to speak to them. I had to leave to meet someone — an appointment."

Janet glanced swiftly at the girl. She had a strong feeling that the Portuguese was keeping something back — something vital!

"And how can you be so sure that this man and Alison were — were lovers?" she pressed. "Did something else happen to give you that impression?"

Magdalena stared hard into Janet's face, disdain flickering in the lovely dark eyes. "Do all English women know so little of love?"

"Please — Senorita — " Janet chose to disregard the childish insinuation. "About this man — tell me what you know of him."

Magdalena sighed and lifted her hair from her face with long, polished fingers. "For days Alison had been like the mouse. She would not speak, or laugh, or do anything that was fun. I make joke with her one day and say that I think she is in love. But she look at me with strange eyes and she say, "Magdalena, some people may call it love, but how can it be so?"

The lovely girl paused and moved nearer to the window to look out.

"Please," Janet prompted, "do go on, Senorita."

Magdalena turned back again with a rather bored smile. "Do you not find those words strange?"

Janet nodded but didn't comment further.

"I thought them very strange words and I ask her to tell me what she means by them. What man had made her feel like that? Was it this new lover? But she laugh at Magdalena and say no, it was not he. Then, when I asked her to tell me more of him, I could see how angry she had grown."

"Angry?" Janet asked in surprise.

Magdalena nodded. "Yes, very angry!

It was then that we had our argument. She tell me to — how you say — mind my own business!" She squared her slim shoulders and glared at Janet scornfully. "To say that to me is the insult! I allow no-one to speak to me like that! She had made me so angry that I slap her face. Then she run out of apartment and I hear her say to Maria that she is going back to Camacha."

"Camacha? To the children's home?" Janet said.

But Magdalena wasn't listening and her voice grew more petulant as she went on. "How could she say such a thing to me? I was her friend!" The black eyes narrowed as they swung to Janet. "But I do not think she went to Camacha at all! I think perhaps she went to her new lover at Cabo Girao."

Janet's adrenalin was flowing now. At last, she was getting somewhere!

"How do you know he lives at Cabo Girao? You must know more about him if you know that much!"

"No!" Magdalena replied hotly. "I know nothing!"

"Can you tell me his name?" Janet persisted eagerly. "Did he ever visit my sister? Can you describe him to me?"

"I see him at the club for one moment, that is all." She shrugged. "He is not as handsome as our Portuguese men — too light. For me, my men must be — "

Magdalena broke off abruptly as the telephone rang again and, excusing herself, Janet crossed the room to answer it. She listened to the voice of the desk clerk telling her that Pedro from the Senor Perestrelo's estate was waiting for her and would she go down immediately."

"Tell him I'll be down in five minutes, please." Janet replied, then replaced the receiver and glanced at her watch. José had told her he would pick her up at ten o'clock and it was not yet nine-thirty.

She turned back to Magdalena. "Would you excuse me, Senorita

Vieira? Thank you for coming to see me and I'll certainly go up to Cabo Girao, but right now someone is waiting for me downstairs."

Magdalena spun to face her, her dark eyes wide with astonishment. "Who is downstairs?"

"José Perestrelo and I have arranged to go to Camacha this morning, but — "

"You go with José?" the dark-eyed girl demanded.

"Well, I was supposed to," Janet explained softly, "but it's Pedro — his manager — who has come for me."

Magdalena's composure completely deserted her and she took a few hurried steps towards the door. As she reached it she turned back, staring at Janet with eyes now filled with alarm.

"Do not tell him I was here," she begged. "I shall deny it! I shall deny everything!"

"All right, if that's how you want it," Janet agreed, more than a little perplexed.

Halfway through the door, Magdalena hesitated. "You will find Alison at Cabo Girao but do not tell anyone that I have told you!"

Then with a final flourish, she flounced out of the room.

8

WHEN Janet went downstairs a little while later, she found Pedro talking amiably to Jack and Mildred Furness who were taking coffee in the hotel lounge and, as she entered, he rose to meet her.

"Senorita Robinson," he said, his English amazingly good, "I believe you know Mr and Mrs Furness?"

Janet nodded vaguely as he explained his presence. "José is delayed and sends his apologies. I will take you to your destination."

"Will he be meeting me at Camacha later?"

He smiled blandly. "He did not say. Come, my car is outside."

He turned to the two people seated at the table. "Mrs and Mrs Furness, excuse us please, we must leave now."

"Of course." The soft grey eyes

of Mildred Furness fixed on Janet. "Perhaps we will see you at dinner? Maybe you will join us?"

"Yes, thank you. I'll look forward to it."

They said their goodbyes and, as they came down the steps of the hotel and into the car park, Janet felt the cold pinpricks of rain still blowing in the wind. The sky was overcast and the mountains all around were obscured by thick banks of grey cloud.

Pedro noticed her upwards glance and remarked, "Storms like this are quite usual at this time of the year — it will not last long."

Janet nodded but made no effort to reply. She was conscious of only one thing and that was that she must get this visit to the children's home at Camacha over with as quickly as she could and make her way to Cabo Girao. She felt a stab of disappointment too, that Magdalena had shown such alarm at the mention of José Perestrelo's name and prayed that he was not mixed up in this business of her sister.

She smiled inwardly — a small, rueful smile. Careful now, she told herself silently. You hardly know the man. And attractive or not, you don't know what he could be capable of.

They drove in silence, the signs of Camacha swooping by. Janet huddled deeper in the seat, wary of Pedro's speed and of the alarming curves on the mountain road. She closed her eyes as they hurtled through a small, huddled village, and then opened them again to glance at the arrogant tilt to the estate-manager's chin.

Pedro was far from handsome. His hair was thick, greying and unruly, his eyes small, deepset and heavily browed. Probably somewhere in his forties, he was grossly overweight and this gave the impression that he was much older than he actually was. A faint gleam of sweat was covering his cheekbones and his nostrils flared above a narrow upper lip.

He thrust his foot down harder on

the accelerator and Janet gasped as the car hurtled round yet another sharp zig-zagging curve.

"Afraid?" he said then laughed cruelly.

"What's the rush?"

He laughed again but gave no answer and it was some time before she realised that they were no longer on the road that would take them to Camacha. This road was taking them even farther into the mountains, and the swirling mist was already shrouding the trees on either side of them.

"Where are we going?" she asked warily.

"We're almost there now."

"Almost where?"

The man's swarthy face remained impassive, his concentration fixed on the twisting road ahead.

"Pedro, I insist that you tell me where we are going," she demanded. "This isn't the road for Camacha."

"I did not say we were going to Camacha."

Suddenly, Janet felt vaguely nervous and she threw the foreman a quick, anxious glance. "Pedro! Please! Tell me where we are going."

He threw her a look that unnerved her even more. "When something gets in the way it has to be got rid of, yes? Now, I wish to concentrate on the driving Senorita. Please do not ask any more questions."

They began to descend steeply, coming out of the mist into a valley and Janet knew now that Pedro had other plans in mind. They jolted over a narrow bridge that spanned a fast-flowing river and, all at once, she felt trapped. There was no sign of life. No sign of anything except the forbidding mountains all around.

"What's going on, Pedro? What is this all about?"

"Just a few more minutes and we will be there. Be patient."

Soon they were weaving down the hillside, passing trellises of vines, and crops of sweet potatoes. When they had almost reached the bottom, Pedro turned sharply into a narrow gateway and Janet could see that they were making for one of the red-roofed farmhouses that were scattered all over the island. A man was working in a nearby field and, as they approached, he straightened up raising his hand in recognition.

Pedro waved back.

He swung the car into a grove of sugar cane and drew up in front of a white-painted door. The sun came out momentarily, it's brilliance dazzling Janet's eyes but, when Pedro switched off the engine and the sun disappeared again behind a cloud, the whole scene suddenly took on a more sombre and forbidding aspect.

"It is the Casa das Torres."

"Why are we here?"

"Because it is remote. It is perfect when you have something to hide, yes?" He smiled faintly. "Do not worry, Senorita, you will be quite comfortable — for now."

Janet gripped the edge of her seat, terrified now as she turned wide, frightened eyes towards Pedro.

"Are you kidnapping me? How long do you intend to keep me here?"

"Do not ask so many questions."

"How long do you intend to play this little game?" she demanded hotly, ignoring his order.

"For as long as it is necessary."

"But why? What's the point? You can't do this! I'll walk back to Funchal!"

He laughed softly. "No, Senorita, you will not do that. You would get lost in the mountains."

Janet sat back in angry frustration. "But, why? Why keep me here? What good will it do you?"

"We keep you here until our business is concluded. After that — " He shrugged, grinning widely and exposing wide-gapped, yellow teeth. "You should not have come looking for your sister."

"My sister!" She grabbed his arm

eagerly. "Is Alison here?"

This time he laughed outright, but then the amusement died as he snarled, "No Senorita Janet. She is staying with a friend of mine until we decide what to do with her."

"At Cabo Girao?"

He turned menacingly towards her. "What do you know of Cabo Girao? Who told you of that place?"

"I — I don't know — I must have heard it some — "

"You do know of it!" he interrupted savagely. "You know too much! Now you have also become too troublesome. But it makes no difference — you will both be dealt with when our business is safely at an end." Then a movement caught his eye and he turned away. "Ah, here is Filipa."

Janet jerked her head towards the farm. A black-garbed woman had appeared in the doorway and Janet turned to study her briefly. It was hard to tell her age; she could have been anywhere between fifty and seventy but as Pedro pushed open the door of the car, she knew it was time to make a try for freedom. Either that, or be a prisoner like her sister.

Her eyes slid to the keys still in the ignition as Pedro pulled on the handbrake, but it seemed an age before he finally opened the door. He lurched himself forward straddling his legs outside the car and straightening up, calling out something in Portuguese to the woman.

Then, taut as a wire and breathing fast, Janet swung herself into the driver's seat and shoved the handbrake off, opening the throttle with a roar. There was a shout and a curse and Janet jerked the car sharply forward — too sharply. The car stalled, and that one fumbling moment cost her dearly as Pedro pushed her roughly from the wheel and grabbed the keys, laughing now and dangling them in front of her nose.

"Do not try to be clever, Senorita.

You will get hurt."

"I insist that you take me back to Funchal!"

But Pedro merely laughed and thrust the keys deep into his pocket. "Such spirit have the English girls."

He grabbed her upper arm roughly and pulled her from the car, pushing her forwards. Then, with his hand still firmly gripped around her arm, they walked up to the house.

When they reached the door, Janet tried again to seize an opportunity. "Senora! I have been brought here against my will. I wish to go back to Funchal."

The only response from the woman was a bright, gaping smile as she beckoned Janet into the house.

"You are wasting your time," Pedro told her in an amused tone. "Filipa speaks no English!"

Angrily, Janet turned on him. "Why are you doing this? And what have you done to my sister?"

"It is the price you must pay for your

sister's interference. Now, go inside, please."

He pushed her forward again and Janet stumbled inside the house, realising that at this point at least, there was little sense in arguing further. All she could hope for now was a chance to, somehow, get hold of the car keys again and drive away from this god-forsaken place in one piece.

Filipa beckoned again and Janet followed reluctantly. It could have been a beautiful house if the dismal light outside would brighten, but Janet was seeing it only in fear and, to her, it seemed cold, uncomfortable and ominous.

The woman led her up the solid staircase and turned twice along the galleries until she reached a door and opened it. And, as Janet stepped inside and looked around, she realised that no matter how clean and welcoming Filipa had tried to make it, it was nonetheless to be her prison.

Filipa stood watching her from the

doorway and Janet forced out a few words of Portuguese, "Senora. Help me! Please, help me!"

Her efforts were rewarded by yet another gaping, toothless smile, followed by a string of words which meant nothing to her, and when the woman turned away, Janet's heart sank even further as Pedro came into the room.

He came up close, his arm reaching out like a bar of steel and pulling her towards him. Janet shut her eyes, vaguely wondering if he intended to kill her there and then as she felt his hot, rapid breathing against her cheek.

She pulled away in an involuntary movement of resistance, but he sensed it and his arms closed brutally around her, an ugly light blazing in his eyes.

"Do not be so cold, my English rose," he said through gritted teeth. "Your stay here with Pedro could be very nice — "

She jerked away from his hot, searching lips and he said again, in a tone of mock reproach. "Ah, you will regret that. Pedro can make you very happy — "

Suddenly. Janet wanted to be sick. She wondered, hysterically, why it should be that a man who meant her so much harm could expect her to kiss him. Swift anger took the place of terror and she kneed him hard in the groin, sending him screaming back against the door.

He cried out in agony and, her eyes wild, Janet grabbed the first thing that came to hand, a carafe from the bedside table.

She held it theateningly above her head.

"Don't you dare touch me!" she yelled. "Keep your filthy hands off me!"

He gave another, ugly laugh. "You will change your mind about Pedro when you have been here a little longer."

He laughed again as he closed the door behind him and Janet's heart sank even lower when she heard the scraping sound as he turned the key. She was locked in!

She ran across to the window in a jerk of panic. There had to be a way out of here. There had to be! She must somehow get back to Funchal and inform the police. But, as she stood looking out at the mountains, she knew she was in for no easy task.

Janet set herself down on the bed, her body tense and her face without a trace of colour. She gripped her hands tightly together on her lap. What a fool she'd been! How could anyone be so crazy and allow a man to abduct her so easily? Why, she'd got into Pedro's car without even questioning it. She'd been taken completely off guard.

Her mind went to José Perestrelo. Had he sent Pedro? Was he behind all this? Had he set it up to get her out of the way? No wonder her sister's fear had been so stark in the unfinished letter. These were dangerous — and unscrupulous — people.

What was behind it all? What good

would it do anybody to keep her prisoner like this?

Janet heard voices coming from downstairs and she got up and pounded on the door.

"Let me out!" she shouted. "Let me out of here!" But it was no use. Soon, the voices faded and she heard the sound of the car as Pedro drove away.

She slumped back on the bed, her eyes enormous in her pale face. For a long time she lay trying to gather her wits and to formulate a way of escape. Vague ideas fitted through her troubled mind, only to vanish again as she realised their futility.

After a while, she got up and went over to the window, shading her eyes against the sun's light. She tried to open it, but it was locked. Her eyes ranged the grey-shadowed chain of mountains and, even in her troubled state, she could not help but marvel at the beauty of it.

Then something caught her eye. High

up, running horizontally along the craggy side of the mountain, something glinted in the light. No, it wasn't a road, it was a water course. Her hopes rose as she followed its route with her eyes. Wherever there was a watercourse there had to be a path — and where there was a path . . . Surely, it would lead her to a village.

Her heart thudded now as she recognised this as her means of escape, but her first priority was to find a way out of the house. She glanced at her watch, feeling a small shock of surprise to find that it was still morning — still only a little after eleven-fifteen.

9

STRUNG up with tension, Janet sat propped against the pillows with her legs hunched under her chin trying desperately to think of a way out of this awful mess. There had to be something she could do. There just had to be!

Impatiently, she swung her legs off the bed and crossed to the window, her eyes once more taking in the breathtaking view as they drifted hopefully upwards towards the gleaming watercourse — so near — yet so far away!

When she heard the scraping of a key again, a quick glance at her watch told her it was exactly twelve noon.

She turned nervously to see Filipa coming through the door. The woman nodded, smiling at Janet and chattering away in Portuguese as she placed a small vase of fresh flowers on the bedside table. Janet smiled back, tightly, and reining in her frustrated anger. She had no idea what the woman was saying, nor did she much care. But then, through the torrent of incomprehensible words, a couple of normally insignificant ones suddenly sparked off a signal to her brain.

"*Comer — comer — lanche.*"

Janet's heart did a double turn. "Lunch? Food?"

Filipa beamed toothlessly and nodded. The woman had moved back to the door and was beckoning for Janet to follow and so, with a grateful smile, she followed her downstairs.

From the stairway Janet had a good view of the main door and, her eyes darting to it, she felt a swift surge of relief to see that the key was still in the lock. She could make a dash for it! She could easily overcome the frail little woman who had been left as her guard.

Then, as Janet entered the quaint,

rose-tiled dining-room, she hesitated, her eyes moving furtively to the window. In the distance, she could see the man, Jaime Pedro had called him, still at his work in the potato field and she realised that if she tackled Filipa now, he could be a problem.

What little she'd learned of the Portuguese woman was the fact that, as small as she was, she had a voice like a banshee, and the fuss she would be sure to kick up would most certainly alert him.

No, she must play this carefully. Somehow, she had to think of some-thing that would lower Filipa's guard; prevent her from making too much noise; and, at the same time, give her enough leeway to make a run for it.

As she salt herself down, Janet's brain stepped up a gear.

She nibbled on some bread, her eyes darting everywhere and, in the next few tension-filled seconds, Janet formed a plan. When she was sure Filipa was not looking she unclasped the slim red belt from around her waist and slipped it into her pocket then, quite casually, she picked up one of the linen napkins and unfolded it letting it hang loosely from her hand. A tough situation demanded tough measures.

Bracing herself and feigning a small cry of pain, she clutched her stomach.

"Filipa!" she choked. "Please! *Agradar*! Water! *Agua*!"

Filipa's bony arms flew up in consternation and she rushed across to see what was the matter. Within seconds Janet had grabbed at the back of the woman's head, pulling it towards her and stuffing the napkin firmly between the protesting lips. With the gag firmly in place she plunged her right leg into Filipa's stomach, winding her and bringing her face downwards to the floor. Then she grabbed at the thin wrists, pulling the belt from her pocket and — none to gently — tied Filipa's thin hands firmly behind her back.

Tying a final knot on the napkin, Janet then rolled the woman over, making sure she could breathe. And, although Filipa made a brave attempt to free herself, the muffled protests soon faded and she lay back again, her black, uncomprehending eyes staring wildly.

"I'm sorry, Filipa," Janet whispered, giving a final check on the belt before straightening up and making for the door. "I didn't want to do this to you, but if you mix with such people what else can you expect? As for me, I'm getting out of here."

Janet turned swiftly and, moving as quietly and as quickly as she could she ran out of the dining-room and made for the door, turning the key and edging herself outside. If Jaime looked up now he would see her, so keeping her head down and staying close to the shrubs, she headed for the narrow track at the back of the farm.

First running, and then slowing to a fast walk, it took her a little over ten minutes to reach it, and she kept on going until she felt sure that she had put a fair distance between herself and the house before she slowed her pace.

Once clear of the vineyards she looked back, satisfied now that no-one would see her.

She began her climb towards the watercourse, the sun's heat sending a shimmer across the valley and wrapping it in a baking stillness. From her vantage point on the rise she could still see the roof of Casa das Torres and she shivered in spite of the heat. She mustn't stop. If she lingered, they would still have time to catch up with her.

She rested a minute more then moved on. With the ground firm and easy beneath feet she made good progress, figuring that as long as she stayed close against the rock's face she was in no danger. The slope at this point wasn't very steep and gauzy insects danced above her head.

After fifteen minutes of hard, determined effort, she reckoned she must have ascended at least a good three hundred feet. It seemed as good a route as any and, she reasoned, there was always a chance that, sooner or later, she would come across someone who could help her get back to Funchal.

Soon, the sound of water became louder. And, as she rounded yet another bend in the mountainside she came at last upon the watercourse. At this point it was more like a tumbling waterfall and it soon wet her through with the spray. Her clothes clung to her skin and, moments later, she felt quite cold as the clouds moved across the sun, pushed by a strong breeze that was blowing in from the sea.

Farther on, the watercourse turned sharply, disappearing into one of the deep, dark fissures of the mountains. There was nothing else for Janet to do now but to take the narrow track around it — a track similar to the one José had carried her over on their way to the orphanage.

She paused, scared stiff at the prospect and, gritting her chattering teeth, she considered the alternative. Was it possible that she could wade through the cutting and so avoid the terrifying prospect of balancing on just three feet of path with nothing between her and eternity? She glanced down and, within seconds, her head had already begun to spin from the steep drop below. That was enough to convince her. She would take her chances in the tunnel!

Taking a deep breath, she stepped gingerly into the swift-flowing water and waded forward. It was bitterly cold and came well above her knees. Balancing herself, she took another step and pushed on towards the gap to squeeze her way through, then, slowly but surely, she inched along the tunnel until, after ten minutes or so, she finally emerged from the other side, blinking in the dazzling glare of daylight.

Drenched, but grateful for her good fortune, she rested for a minute on the soft, dry grass and let the sun's rays warm her freezing body. Then, relief flowing through her that she had made it this far, she moved on again.

Half a mile or so farther on — and to Janet's utter despair — the watercourse narrowed once more and, this time, there was no tunnel. The water surged between the rocks leaving no room for anyone, not even of her own slender build. This time, she had no option but to take the path around it and, as she gazed across the narrow space, her heart sank into utter desperation. This path was even more precarious. A sheer drop which fell away, leaving her terrified of the consequences should she make the slightest slip.

Janet sank down on to a boulder, holding her head in her hands. She would never make it this time! She looked up again, her eyes filled with frustration and despair, remembering Pedro's confident boast that she would never make it back along through the mountains to the village.

Yet she knew, somehow, she must!

Somehow, she must summon up the courage to overcome this obstacle if she was to make it to Funchal. So, slowly, her knees trembling, she rose to her feet and moved forward again.

Petrified, she almost over-balanced as a wave of vertigo overcame her. Then, resolutely, she dredged up her courage and edged on to the path, clinging to the sides of the rock for dear life. Step by painful step, she inched herself along, even more fearful now of her growing inner panic. She kept her head up and her eyes straight ahead, praying that the path would widen soon.

But, it was not to be. As she turned the corner, hoping it was the end of her ordeal, yet another ledge stretched before her, and this one was even narrower than the last.

At this point, Janet knew she had two choices. She could either go forward or retrace her steps. Either way was a death trap. And now, drenched in the frozen sweat of fear and gripped by sheer, blind panic, she rested her burning cheek against the dry rock face. There was no longer anything she could do. Her numbed brain was paralysed, refusing to send instructions to her limbs — she could no longer move a muscle.

Time meant nothing to her now. Fiercely, she forced her frozen brain into some form of action, but each time she tried to move herself, the paralysis set in even deeper.

Then she heard it. A sound. A voice.

At first she thought her panic-stricken head was imagining it, but when it came again she knew it was real. Relief flooded through her as she heard the sound coming from some distance away. It didn't matter anymore who it was. Someone was here to save her!

"Janet! Janet! For goodness' sake, where are you?"

In that fearful moment the sound she was now hearing was the most wonderful she had ever heard in her life. It was the voice of José!

When Janet tried to call out she couldn't move her lips. Her throat was tight, constricted, and she could make no sound. She remained crouched against the overhanging rock, tightening her hold on the life-saving crevice as the water flowed from within the mountain, its sound from this distance almost like a whimper.

"Janet!" José's voice came again. "Answer me! Please, Janet. Answer me!"

Janet tried desperately to respond but all she could manage was a dry croak.

"Oh, please," she prayed, "don't let him give up on me and go away."

"Janet! Janet!"

The sound was closer now, echoing off the bare rock face. And when José finally came into her view, his image was so sudden that it startled her. With the clouds blown away, the sharp edge of the rock was etched against the blinding blueness of the sky and there, in the distance, Janet watched as the dark figure moved nearer, taking the precarious ledge in his stride as though it was a hundred foot wide.

When he was near enough to see her he came to a dead halt.

"It's all right," he called soothingly. "Stay quite still. Don't try to move — just stay exactly as you are."

Janet couldn't have moved even if she'd wanted to. With a feeling that was half joy, half sick fear, she watched as he came towards her, talking all the while in a gentle, reassuring tone, and when at last he came within reach, she was suddenly galvanised into action and stretched out her arm in thankfulness.

"No. Don't move!" He instructed with a sharp firmness. "Stay right there! Don't move an inch!"

He edged himself forward until he reached her side, raising a warning hand.

"Come, take my hand."

Janet reached out in a desperate hope for safety.

"Slowly — slowly — " His hand held on to her tightly then slackened, moving upwards to grasp her wrist.

"I — I can't — " Suddenly her teeth were chattering uncontrollably.

"Yes, you can. It's OK, I've got you. Now, slowly, come towards me."

Janet edged gingerly along the ledge.

"There," he said quietly. "That's it."

Careful not to look down over the edge, Janet followed as José edged his way along. He moved steadily and carefully, his strong hand guiding her to safety. His low voice soothed her with words of reassurance.

"You'll be safe soon. Don't worry. It's OK, I'm here. Take your time, cara . . . "

10

JOSÉ moved on carefully, continuing along the path. Beside them, and once they were beyond the fissure, the water burbled quietly on and, when she summoned up enough courage to look around her, Janet saw that the path had widened again and a sun-drenched valley lay below them like a vibrant patchwork quilt.

Watching José, she thanked God for his strong and reassuring presence, and for his incredible bravery that had surely saved her life.

At last, José came to a stop.

"I — I — was so scared," she whispered. "I could hardly believe it when I heard your voice."

He stared down, the tension of the last half hour clearly visible in his eyes. "What made you do such a crazy thing? You could have killed yourself."

131

"I know . . . but what else could I do? I had to get away somehow — "

"You should have waited!" he broke in, gripping her shoulders and shaking her a little. "Surely you knew I would come for you."

"But — I didn't — I didn't know if you knew where I was, or — or — " Janet broke off, gazing up at him and a slight touch of defiance crept into her tone.

"Or what?" he demanded.

"I didn't know if it was your idea that Pedro — that Pedro — "

He stared at her in utter disbelief. "You're surely not serious?"

"I didn't want to believe it. But so many bad things have happened lately — to my sister and, now, to me — I didn't know what to believe," Janet faltered miserably. "I'm sorry if I — "

José gave a deep, resigned sigh. "I suppose it's quite understandable," he conceded brusquely, then, more gently, added, "Come on, we'd better make a move."

They set off along the track, Janet following behind and still shaky from her ordeal on the path.

"But how did you know where I was?" she asked. "How did you know that I would be up on the mountain?"

"I'll tell you on the way down. We're not far from Cabo Girao and there's someone there I'd like you to meet."

★ ★ ★

They began their descent into the valley and, stopping now and then for Janet to catch her breath, José began to tell her of the things that had happened since he left her at the hotel the night before. And what he had discovered that had brought him to Casa das Torres in such haste.

"As I said, I telephoned the matrona and, at last, she told me what was going on up there," he said grimly, striding along the path and holding Janet's still-shaking hand. "It wasn't as hard as I thought. She was too scared to try to hide it any longer."

"Scared of what?" Janet urged. "Pedro? Was she scared of Pedro?"

"Yes. And of me and Bill, not to mention the authorities."

"Bill? Who's Bill?"

"You'll meet him soon enough. Anyway, she realised that it was all over and, hoping to save her own neck, she started to talk. She told me the whole sordid story." His face has darkened now with pent-up anger. "I knew something was wrong at the orphanage but, how blind I must have been this last month."

"Blind to what? José . . . please . . . what's been going on? Have you found out anything about my sister? Please, tell me. I can't bear this mystery any longer."

"You won't have to. Come, we're almost there."

The track had widened and was now a road, and soon they were winding their way through the narrow, dusty streets of a small town. In truth, it was hardly more than a large village and Janet held on to José's arm as he led her towards a pretty, pink-washed cottage.

Within minutes of their approach, a door opened to reveal a tall, blond man who was already greeting them in the slow, southern drawl of an American.

"José!" The man grinned. "Glad you could make it!"

"Only by the skin of our teeth." José grinned back, grasping the man's hand and shaking it vigorously. "Well, here she is, Bill. I'd like you to meet Janet at last, although she almost didn't make it. Janet, this is my friend, Bill McIvor."

They shook hands and then the man turned, calling to someone back in the house. "Alison! Honey! We got company!"

"Alison?" Janet could hardly believe her ears. "My sister's here?"

She turned expectantly towards the darkened doorway as, moments later and just visible in the shadows, another figure emerged — the slight, familiar shape of Alison.

With a delighted cry, Janet sprang forward. "Alison!"

The two girls hugged each other, dancing around in a little, excited circle.

"Oh, Alison." Janet laughed. "I thought I'd never find you. Are you all right?"

"I'm fine. Oh, Janet, you don't know how good it is to see you."

"I've been so worried — " Janet began. "I can't believe it's really you! Oh, let me hug you again — "

The sisters' joy in finding each other safe and sound continued for some minutes more until, when the excitement had finally subsided, José put an arm around each of them and led them inside the house. Once inside, still reeling from the joy of their reunion and still holding tightly to Alison's hand, Janet turned to look at him, shaking her head and asking quietly, "Now, please, do you think one of you could tell me just what's been going on?"

"Oh, Janet, you'll never believe it!" Alison exclaimed, moving across to a wooden dresser and setting a jug of wine on to the table. "If it hadn't been for Bill and José, I don't know what would have happened to me."

"From my recent experience, I've a pretty good idea." She smiled again and looked up at the tall American, adding, "Bill McIvor — you're the mystery man, I take it."

The American laughed as he reached for four glasses. "Hardly a mystery. All I did was to come here to spend a nice, quiet, relaxing vacation with an old buddy of mine and look what happened!"

"That's exactly what I'm waiting to hear."

He filled a glass with the wine and handed it to her. "I end up — not only meeting the best-looking gal I ever set eyes on — but spend half of my time helping my buddy get her out of trouble." He grinned fondly at Alison and winked his eye at José, then he turned back to Janet, adding jokingly, "Not to mention double-trouble when you came along. Lucky for all of you that I happened to stop by, huh?"

Janet smiled wryly as she regarded the tall American. "That still doesn't tell me anything except the fact that you're old friends — you and José?"

"We go back a long way. We were at college together in Houston. And I was looking forward to taking in a spot of fishing with him again but, instead, when I arrived here I couldn't get him away from that kids' home of his. And I could see that something was biting him."

"That's true enough," José admitted, "something was."

Bill slapped him on the back and filled his glass. "You should know better than to try to keep things from your old pal. I tried to get it out of him but all he would say was that he could be wrong. That was really bugging."

"I had no proof," José murmured,

"but Bill kept on until I had finally told him that I felt there had to be something wrong up there. Then, when I told him, he decided to do some investigating for himself."

Bill shrugged. "That's what comes of being a cop, I guess."

"But what made you suspect that there was something wrong, José?" Janet asked.

He shook his head. "Just a feeling! The matrona, for instance, and the way she would put me off going through the files unless she was there with me to see what I was looking at. And the way she would put off any visitors unless they made a specific appointment. It never used to be like that — it has always been an open place."

"But surely, it had to be more than that."

"Yes, it was. My grandfather received a letter from the police in Lisbon asking if he knew anything of a baby who had been kidnapped — if it had been placed in the orphanage."

"Why should they think that? Had they some suspicion that the orphanage had been used for that purpose before?"

"Apparently, yes. But we weren't to know that until much later. Anyway, he was very upset by the letter and asked me to look into it. When I went up to the orphanage to check on the names of the new children, Pedro was there and, when I asked him if anyone had contacted them about a child that was not on our list, I could see he was clearly agitated. When I asked the matrona to show me the records, he insisted on showing them to me himself."

José paused, his face drawn and white. "It wasn't his job and when I pointed that fact out to him, he said that the matrona had been ill lately and had got behind with things — that he'd been looking after the records himself, as a favour to her."

"And did you believe him?"

"Of course not. But I had no real proof that he was involved at that stage." José took a sip of wine and glanced at Janet bleakly. "After that, I kept an eye on things and, when Alison disappeared — well, that really left me with a bad taste in the mouth." He looked directly at Janet, adding sombrely, "As a matter of fact, Janet, you confirmed my suspicions."

"I did? In what way?"

"When you mentioned that Alison had told you in her letters that there were babies at the orphanage. I was convinced that my worst fears were about to be realised. We only ever took children of school age — my grandfather undertook their education — the tiny ones were always taken to Funchal." He frowned. "Naturally, I had to get to the bottom of it."

"They told him I'd met someone and gone off to get married." Alison grinned ruefully. "They even forced me to write a note."

Bill squeezed Alison's hand reassuringly and carried on with the account. "When José told me about it I thought it was time for a little professional intervention. I don't like to see a buddy worried, so I decided to do a bit of nosing around myself."

"And that's how you met my sister?" Janet asked.

He glanced at Alison with another fond grin. "Not right away. She'd already disappeared by then and I believed what everyone said — that she'd gone off with some guy."

"What did make you leave the orphanage, Alison?"

Hands shaking, Alison picked up her glass and sipped a little of the wine. "I didn't suspect anything at first," she began, "I thought — "

She almost faltered and Bill's strong hand gave her another reassuring squeeze.

"Don't get upset, honey," he said softly. "It's all over now, thank goodness."

"But what exactly has been going on?" Janet pressed in bewilderment. "And why should Pedro want to kidnap me — and you, too, Alison?"

"I'll explain," José said, drawing a chair up by Janet's side and letting his arm slide around her shoulder.

"It all started about a year ago," he began quietly. "It seems Pedro had read of a couple in Lisbon who were desperate for a child and, for some reason or other, were refused adoption. His sister had a child — illegitimate — a boy a couple of months old. And he knew she couldn't afford to keep it so he persuaded her to sell it to this couple — "

Janet's eyes widened in disbelief. "You mean he sold his own nephew?"

"I'm afraid so," José muttered icily. "But don't shed too many tears. Apparently, they both made a nice profit from the transaction and they realised the potential of the market. They were as bad as each other. If the kid's new parents were decent, then I reckon the poor little thing got the best out of the deal."

Janet felt suddenly sick as realisation dawned. "Illegal adoption?"

José nodded grimly.

"But, surely," she argued, "surely, the adoptive parents could sense something was wrong? That it was all too easy?"

"It's amazing what lengths some couples will go to for a child of their own and Pedro and his sister cashed in on it. Sadly, there are plenty of unmarried girls in Madeira who are too ashamed to tell their parents of their trouble. And, unknown to me, or my grandfather, Pedro — with his sister as his partner and the matrona on his payroll — arranged for these poor girls to stay at the orphanage until after the babies were born."

"But how did he manage to find the prospective parents without raising too much suspicion?"

"He covered that, too. Money talks, you know, and he found a couple to act as agents. It was their job to find places for them with the rich couples in Lisbon and Oporto."

Janet shook her head, murmuring,

"How awful — and how sad."

She glanced up at Bill who had moved to sit on the arm of Alison's chair, his tanned arm resting loosely across her sister's shoulders in the intimate way of a couple more than just fond of one another.

"And what part did you play, Bill?" she asked. "How did your nosing around lead you to Alison? How did she come to be here at Cabo Girao? I have a feeling that you're right in the thick of it."

"I sure am," he admitted grinning widely. "I became a star player when we laid our little trap — "

"Damn! Damn Pedro!" José muttered. "I trusted him — and this is the way he repays me!"

11

JOSÉ rose and helped himself to more wine from the jug. The skin was tight across his cheekbones and something like hatred shone in his eyes.

"Don't let it get to you, José," Bill murmured. "You couldn't have known — nobody could."

Janet shivered slightly. The sun had gone down and the room felt cold.

"Please," she said, "tell me what happened next. How did you set your trap for Pedro?"

Bill emptied his glass and leaned over to pour himself another. "José and I talked it over — "

He broke off as José cut him off with a motion of one hand.

"I'll tell her," he said.

José held Janet's gaze, grave and serious, before continuing with the story. "We decided to work together, Bill and I, to try to get to the bottom of it all. Just by chance, one night after dinner, and when I was busy on some papers in my study, Bill managed to get into conversation with Pedro — "

"He was out back clearing some brushwood and I offered to give him a hand," Bill explained.

"That's right." José went on, "Bill told Pedro that he was in financial trouble back home and had come to Madeira to burn some money out of me — his rich college buddy. But it hadn't worked. I had refused to help. And now he was pretty desperate and had to get hold of some money quickly before the mob he was pretending to work for finished him off for good."

Bill grinned. "Pretty impressive, huh? I think I should take up screen writing. Hollywood would pay a fortune for my inventiveness."

José smiled at last, a sort of relieved little quirk of the mouth. "Very impressive, Bill." José looked to Bill to continue.

"Anyway, Pedro swallowed it. He must have believed me because, the next thing, he was telling me how easy it was to pick up a few dollars if you knew where to look." Bill laughed with a kind of contempt. "So I played along. I asked him how, and I couldn't believe my luck when he told me of this little set-up in Madeira — not implicating himself, I might add."

Janet shook her head. "I can imagine. So, what happened then?"

"Well, I must have convinced him because, a couple of days later, he took me on one side and suggested that the States could be a good market. I agreed, of course, but a market for what? Then he told me of a girl who was desperate — her baby was due any day and her parents would throw her out, send her to a convent in disgrace."

"And was that true?"

Bill shrugged, "I guess so."

148

"It was," José confirmed, grimly, "but she was mistaken about her parents. When the baby arrived they accepted it with open arms and there was no question of their daughter being sent away."

He glanced at Bill, "Sorry. I interrupted. Do go on."

Bill shrugged again. "It's OK, where was I up to?"

Janet prompted him. "You were saying that Pedro was interested in America."

"Oh, yes. Then he asked if I would like to act as his agent in the States — that there must be a good supply from the South — " He broke off with another hard, angry laugh. "He swore me to secrecy, of course, but he sure was a green amateur. He hadn't even checked me out."

Janet gasped. "And what did you say to that?"

Bill shrugged easily. "I played along. I told him, sure I was interested. That there must be thousands of illegitimate babies going begging in South America, and couples in the north who would pay a fortune to adopt a kid, and would he cut me in."

José gave a deep sigh, as though the effort had become too much for him. "When Bill confirmed my suspicions about Pedro, I was sick. I hadn't realised just how big his business had become — was becoming! Anyway, we went along with everything he suggested — me playing ignorance and Bill going along with Pedro."

"And a good job for me you both did." Alison smiled, then looked across at her sister. "You see, Jan, I suspected there was something fishy going on. There had to be something wrong when a pregnant girl would arrive in the dead of night, have a baby, and then go home next day without seeing a doctor, hadn't there?"

Janet nodded. "Yes, there had."

"Then the baby would disappear, too, after a couple of weeks," Alison went on. "And yet, when I asked the matron about it she denied everything — she said that they were just people passing through and that my job was to see to the baby after it was born and that was all!"

Alison's voice became angry. "Did they really believe anyone would swallow that?" She took a deep, composing breath. "Naturally, when every girl who happens to be passing through also happens to be pregnant, and when those same girls also happen to choose that precise moment to have their babies, well, it's a bit too much for anyone to swallow, isn't it?"

Janet nodded sombrely. "Yes, it is. So, what happened?"

"I started to do a bit of snooping and matron caught me one day going through her desk. The next thing she grabbed hold of me — she's a very strong lady — and forced me upstairs to my room and locked me in. Later, Pedro made me write a note about meeting someone and going away with him." She shuddered violently. "Then

151

they took me to that place in the mountains — ”

“I know it well,” Janet avowed darkly, squeezing her sister’s cold hand.

“Well, they kept me there a couple of days,” Alison continued, “and then, out of the blue, Bill came and brought me here.”

Janet turned to Bill McIvor. “And how did you manage that?”

He grinned. “By now I was part of the set-up. I’d made out that I’d found a couple back home who would pay anything they asked for a kid. Anyway, as I’ve already pointed out, Pedro’s not too bright and, seeing only green-backed dollars, he swallowed it. So, when José told me that he believed Pedro had had something to do with Alison’s disappearance, I asked him about it.”

“And?”

“Pedro told me Alison was becoming a nuisance, that she had found out too much and needed to be dealt

152

with, and he'd taken her to Casa das Torres until he'd decided what to do with her. Naturally, I had to do something quick so I suggested that maybe it wasn't a good idea to keep her up there with Filipa. I made out that too many people dropped by — their kin, perhaps — and that it could be risky."

"I saw no-one while I was there," Alison put in softly.

Bill grinned again. "I know that now, honey, but Pedro bought it. He agreed, and it gave me the golden chance to suggest she stayed with me here at Cabo Girao."

Janet glanced from one to the other. "And — and when you went there for Alison — was that the first time you two had met?"

"Sure was. And she only had to look at me once with those baby blue eyes and I was hit like a rocket."

"Before they caught me I almost sent you a letter about it, Jan," Alison confessed, "but I was interrupted and

I never got around to posting it."

"Do you mean the one I found in the photograph frame?"

Alison glanced at Janet in astonishment. "How did you know about that?"

"It doesn't matter now. I'll tell you some other time. Right now I'd be interested to hear how I came to be kidnapped, too. And, even more so, how you knew where I was, José."

"You were already getting too close. They'd heard that you'd been asking questions about Alison so, naturally, they had to get you out of the way, too. When I rang the hotel this morning I was to warn you not to let anyone into your room until I got there, but I was already too late. Imagine how I felt when the desk clerk told me you'd already left with Pedro. I rang Bill and he found out that you'd been taken to the Casa das Torres. God, that was terrible! I thought I might be too late! I drove over straight away only to discover you'd got away ... " A glint of admiration came into his eyes.

"I found Jaime untying Filipa in the kitchen wondering what on earth was happening. They couldn't understand why you had done that to her."

"I hope I didn't hurt her — "

"Only her pride. Apart from that, she's fine."

"Are they in on the baby business?"

He shook his head. "No, they're just an old couple who were told that you were to be Pedro's wife."

Janet turned even paler. "Pedro's wife?"

"Yes, I'm afraid so," he muttered. "You see, in the old days it was quite usual to lock up the bride before the wedding so Filipa thought it was all quite normal. When you tied her up, her only thought was that you would not make a good wife for any man." He paused, smiling a little now and adding ambiguously, "I told her she was wrong, of course."

She twisted to look at him. "Well, thank you."

His smile broadened. "I told her you

would make the perfect wife for the right man. I told her that Pedro had stolen you from me and that I was the right man for you."

"And she believed you?"

"Of course she did. It's the truth, anyway."

Janet's heart stirred, as though wakening from a long sleep and, suddenly, she felt languid and serene. But there were still more questions to be answered.

"But, how did you know I was up on the mountain?"

José laughed softly again and took hold of her hand. "I saw you, well I saw a flash of red and knew it must be you." He gave her hand a squeeze, accompanied by a short, humourless laugh. "I climbed that mountain in record time, I can tell you."

Janet smiled. "I'll always be grateful to you for saving my life, José."

"In Madeira, when you save someone's life, you belong to them for ever."

"Is that so?" she said teasingly.

"Yes, that is so."

They exchanged grins, then Janet asked, "And where is Pedro now?"

"Bill rang the police and they picked him up at the airport, complete with one-way ticket to Lisbon. Who knows where he would have gone from there, but that doesn't matter now. He's in safe hands — Magdalena and the matrona, too."

"Magdalena? She was in it, too?"

Alison nodded vigorously. "Very much so, I'm afraid."

"But in what way?" Janet was even more bewildered. "Magdalena was the one who told me about Cabo Girao. Why should she do that if she was part of the set-up?"

"She must have lost her nerve," Alison answered with a shrug. "She was getting very frightened even when I was with her at the flat. I've found out since that Pedro was threatening her with all sorts of terrible things if she didn't do as he asked. She had already lost her appetite for dirty money, I think, and I can only assume that she was

157

hedging her bets in telling you about Cabo Girao — that it might bode well for her when it all came out."

"And what part did she play in this terrible mess?"

"They paid her to pretend to be the mother," José explained. "The agents would spin a sob story to these desperate people saying that she was being difficult and, in that way, they were able to up the price."

"A lot of the transfers were made at her club," Bill explained. "I found that out by listening in on the extension whenever she rang Pedro. Last week I heard them making arrangements for another delivery and thought we'd got a lucky break at last." He grinned ruefully. "But we missed out on that one, didn't we?" He glanced at José, who nodded his head in wry agreement.

"We missed them by about fifteen minutes," José commented.

"Anyway, we alerted the police and I'd decided to go along, too, with

158

Alison, hoping to catch them in the act, so to speak." He shrugged resignedly. "We were too late. After her show, and by the time we got to her dressing-room, some guy told us she'd already left — an urgent appointment, or something. She must have been tipped off."

Janet's scalp prickled. "Oh, how awful! And these agents — have you found out who they are?"

"Oh, yes, we've known who they are for quite a while," Bill commented scornfully. "But it was a matter of finding something that would nail them. They're a nice, cosy-looking couple who look like butter wouldn't melt in their mouths. They hang out at the hotel as tourists so it was not unusual to see them take a so-called sight-seeing trip to the mainland." He shook his head ruefully. "They had it all worked out — a very clever pair." He glanced across. "You may even know them, Janet — an English couple — Jack and Mildred Furness."

She gasped. "Jack and Mildred Furness!"

In a turmoil of confusion, Janet stood up and went to stand in the doorway and, after an age, she forced herself to say, "I think I've heard enough for one day."

She excused herself and went outside, suddenly feeling the need to be alone in order to gather her thoughts. But, after a moment or two, she heard footsteps behind as Alison came to her side, and the two sisters strolled together to look out over Cabo Girao, the little town that nestled in the amphitheatre of mountains.

"Are you going to marry José, Janet?" Alison asked softly. "He seems very fond of you."

"Yes, Alison, I think I am."

But, even as she answered, Janet knew there was no question in her mind now. She would be José's wife.

"Elliott is nice, but he was never for you, you know."

"I always knew that." Janet linked

her arm into her sister's and regarded her with fond curiosity. "And what about you and Bill?"

"Do you like him?"

"Yes, very much. But, more importantly, do you?"

"Oh, yes. I don't think I've ever met anyone I liked more."

"Then, that's OK." Janet chuckled softly. "I think I'd rather like an American cop for a brother-in-law."

They laughed, then Janet turned as she heard José call her name.

"Janet! It is time for us to go now. Bill and I must give our statements to the police, but you must rest after such a day."

He came up and held her hands, kissing her forehead softly. "And, later, I will come for you at the hotel to take you home."

Back in her hotel room, when Janet had bathed and changed she sat down to write the hardest letter she had ever written in her life.

It was better this way, she reasoned.

161

Breaking the news that she was staying in Madeira — as quickly and as gently as she could — was the kindest way in the end. She knew, too, that Elliott was not a man who would suffer heartbreak at a "Dear John" letter. After all, there had never really been any serious talk of an engagement between them, his career always came before such an emotion as love. And the other things, like the explanation of leaving her job, she would attend to later.

It was a little after nine when José came to pick her up from the hotel for the last time. He smiled briefly and reached for her hand, slipping an emerald ring on to her wedding finger as he said softly, "I have told my grandfather of my love for you and he wishes me to give you this ring."

Janet looked down at the shimmering emerald, her love for José threatening to drown her heart.

"Oh, José — it's — it's beautiful," she whispered.

José smiled. "It is the Perestrelo

bridal ring and it has been in my family for generations. My grandfather is longing for great-grandsons and he is convinced that this ring will ensure the succession."

He kissed the ring then took her in his arms, kissing her with such gentle, possessive passion that Janet's heart was sent soaring with love.

"I love you, Janet," he whispered into her hair. "Will you be my wife?"

Janet smiled up at him, her eyes alight with love. "Yes, José, I will be your wife. After all, you saved my life, so it belongs to you now — and Madeira — for ever. Isn't that what you told me?"

He pulled her closer to him, holding her like a precious child. "And so it shall be, mia querida."

WITH SOMEBODY ELSE
Theresa Charles

Rosamond sets off for Cornwall with Hugo to meet his family, blissfully unaware of the shocks in store for her.

A SUMMER FOR STRANGERS
Claire Hamilton

Because she had lost her job, her flat and she had no money, Tabitha agreed to pose as Adam's future wife although she believed the scheme to be deceitful and cruel.

VILLA OF SINGING WATER
Angela Petron

The disquieting incidents that occurred at the Vatican and the Colosseum did not trouble Jan at first, but then they became increasingly unpleasant and alarming.

DOCTOR NAPIER'S NURSE
Pauline Ash

When cousins Midge and Derry are entered as probationer nurses on the same day but at different hospitals they agree to exchange identities.

A GIRL LIKE JULIE
Louise Ellis

Caroline absolutely adored Hugh Barrington, but then Julie Crane came into their lives. Julie was the kind of girl who attracts men without even trying.

COUNTRY DOCTOR
Paula Lindsay

When Evan Richmond bought a practice in a remote country village he did not realise that a casual encounter would lead to the loss of his heart.

ENCORE
Helga Moray

Craig and Janet realise that their true happiness lies with each other, but it is only under traumatic circumstances that they can be reunited.

NICOLETTE
Ivy Preston

When Grant Alston came back into her life, Nicolette was faced with a dilemma. Should she follow the path of duty or the path of love?

THE GOLDEN PUMA
Margaret Way

Catherine's time was spent looking after her father's Queensland farm. But what life was there without David, who wasn't interested in her?

HOSPITAL BY THE LAKE
Anne Durham

Nurse Marguerite Ingleby was always ready to become personally involved with her patients, to the despair of Brian Field, the Senior Surgical Registrar, who loved her.

VALLEY OF CONFLICT
David Farrell

Isolated in a hostel in the French Alps, Ann Russell sees her fiancé being seduced by a young girl. Then comes the avalanche that imperils their lives.

NURSE'S CHOICE
Peggy Gaddis

A proposal of marriage from the incredibly handsome and wealthy Reagan was enough to upset any girl — and Brooke Martin was no exception.

A DANGEROUS MAN
Anne Goring

Photographer Polly Burton was on safari in Mombasa when she met enigmatic Leon Hammond. But unpredictability was the name of the game where Leon was concerned.

PRECIOUS INHERITANCE
Joan Moules

Karen's new life working for an authoress took her from Sussex to a foreign airstrip and a kidnapping; to a real life adventure as gripping as any in the books she typed.

VISION OF LOVE
Grace Richmond

When Kathy takes over the rundown country kennels she finds Alec Stinton, a local vet, very helpful. But their friendship arouses bitter jealousy and a tragedy seems inevitable.

CRUSADING NURSE
Jane Converse

It was handsome Dr. Corbett who opened Nurse Susan Leighton's eyes and who set her off on a lonely crusade against some powerful enemies and a shattering struggle against the man she loved.

WILD ENCHANTMENT
Christina Green

Rowan's agreeable new boss had a dream of creating a famous perfume using her precious Silverstar, but Rowan's plans were very different.

DESERT ROMANCE
Irene Ord

Sally agrees to take her sister Pam's place as La Chartreuse the dancer, but she finds out there is more to it than dyeing her hair red and looking like her sister.